THE *Royal* ORPHAN

THE *Royal* ORPHAN

Lanelle Thomas

ARCHWAY
PUBLISHING

Archway Publishing books may be ordered through booksellers or by contacting:

Archway Publishing
1663 Liberty Drive
Bloomington, IN 47403
www.archwaypublishing.com
844-669-3957

ISBN: 978-1-4808-9991-9 (sc)
ISBN: 978-1-4808-9992-6 (hc)
ISBN: 978-1-4808-9990-2 (e)

Library of Congress Control Number: 2020923423

Print information available on the last page.

Archway Publishing rev. date: 2/10/2021

To the one who made me a mom
and was as excited as I was to be writing this book.
Love you, Laneah!

CHAPTER 1

"HANNA, ELLENA, THOMAS! DOWNSTAIRS!" MADAM Greer yelled. I finished putting my very few belongings into my bag and swung it over my shoulder. I took one last look around at what had been my bedroom for the last eighteen years, and then I followed Madam Greer's instructions.

Thomas was already waiting at the bottom of the stairs. I joined him and looked around for Hanna. Poor thing was never on time for anything. That was going to make the next part of our lives difficult for her.

You see, in Olandia, the palace went around to all the orphanages every spring to round up those who had not been adopted and had turned eighteen. It was Queen Leona's project to help cut down on the homeless in the country. I thought it was a wonderful idea. I was looking forward to wearing clothes without holes, being fully fed, and getting away from "drear Madam Greer." I felt some pity for her. Running an orphanage could not have been easy, but just because I felt sorry for her did not mean I liked her.

Madame Greer took in a deep breath, about to shout for Hanna again, when she bounded down the stairs.

"Here!" she said. She looked at me and beamed her usual big grin. I smiled back as big as I could, but I knew it was nothing compared to hers.

Hanna was my best friend. As babies, we had both been

abandoned on the doorstep of the orphanage in the dead of winter. Even though I was sad that my mother felt like she could not take care of me, I was grateful she was at least kind enough to leave me at the orphanage instead of abandoning me to the elements.

A knock came at the door. Madame Greer opened it. A palace guard was on the other side.

"I am here to pick up those who have come of age," he stated flatly.

Madame Greer motioned to us. "Here they are, sir."

The guard placed a check in Madame Greer's hand. She smiled widely as she looked at—I am assuming—a large sum.

"Follow me," the guard commanded. We followed him outside, where he led us to a van with five other individuals inside. We climbed in and sat in the empty seats. Hanna and I, of course, found a spot where we could sit by each other.

The guard joined the driver up front, and the van started its path toward the castle.

"You going to miss it?" I asked Hanna as I looked back at the shrinking orphanage.

"Nah. Not much to miss. Are you?"

"Maybe a little. It was a dreary place to grow up, but it holds some good memories for me too."

"Like meeting me?" Hanna said with a flip of her hair.

I giggled. "Of course." I gave her a side hug.

We settled into a comfortable silence as we continued down the road.

The sound of the van's wheels on the ground changed as we went from driving on dirt roads to a paved one. All of us in the van turned to look at the approaching castle.

It was beautiful. It stood three stories high with tannish brick walls and clear glass windows. My heart jumped a little. Part of me still could not believe that was what I was going to call home.

The van came to a stop in front of the huge front steps in the arched driveway.

"Come," the same guard commanded.

We all got out and formed a line behind him. We followed him inside, where he led us to an open room that I presumed was the main hall.

We turned our line to face the king and queen on their thrones. They both smiled at us.

King Olov was a large man, not fat but built. He had a handsome square face with ash-brown hair because of the grays slowly creeping in. He had welcoming brown eyes. Queen Leona was beautiful. She had dark brown, wavy hair that fell a little past her shoulders and kind, brown eyes. I did not think it was possible to feel as comfortable as I was in front of royalty.

"Welcome! I am King Olov, and this is Queen Leona," he said while looking to his wife. "I am sorry that Prince Jonathon could not be here today. He is on diplomatic business. He will return tomorrow."

I could hear Hanna let out a quiet, sad sigh. I knew she was dying to meet the handsome prince.

The king brought forward a gangly, tall man with charcoal-black hair. He looked over our line with an air of superiority. When he met my gaze, I felt nothing but coldness coming from his brown eyes. He gave me a smirk. I quickly looked back to the king.

"This is Hugo, and he will be your supervisor. He will assign you your roles, and then you will be dismissed to get started. Good day." King Olov and Queen Leona stood and took their leave. We all turned our attention to Hugo.

He went down the line, starting at the other end. "You four will follow Henry and get set up as gardeners. You two will follow

Frank and get set up as stable hands. And you two will follow Miriam and get set up for housekeeping."

A short, plump lady came up beside me. She greeted Hanna and me with a smile. "If you will follow me, dearies." As we walked behind her, I could not help but feel I was being watched. I turned to see Hugo staring at me, which made me uncomfortable.

Miriam took us down a flight of stairs to the basement, where many doors lined the hall. "This is the servants' floor," she informed us.

She took us all the way to the end of the hall and pointed to the left door. She looked at Hanna. "That is yours." Then she pointed to the one on the right and looked at me. "And this is yours. Now, there is a uniform in there. Get changed. Pull your hair back. Whatever it is, I don't care, just get your hair off your neck. You will thank me later. When you are done, join me in the main hall again." She turned and left.

Hanna and I looked at each other. She jumped up and down, squealing, "Oh my gosh! We are finally here! I can't believe it! What are you going to do with your hair? Can we be twinsies? Let's be twinsies!"

I smiled. "Sure. Single French braid?"

"Yes!" She turned around and bounded into her room.

I turned and entered my room. To the right was a bed, its top centered against the wall. To the left was a small wooden vanity in the corner and small wooden drawers next to it. I sat my bag down on the bed and opened the top drawer. Inside were three neatly folded, white, long-sleeved shirts and three brown, thick-strapped dresses that came slightly in at the waist and reached the ankles. I took off my old clothes and put on the shirt, followed by the dress. Beside the drawers, on the floor, was a pair of black flats. I put them on. I sat down at the vanity, brushed my hair, and put it back in a French braid.

I looked at myself. I hated my dirty-blonde hair. I felt like my head was indecisive. It did not want to be fully blonde or brunette. I did, however, like my eyes. They were a deep green, like emeralds. I stood and looked at the uniform on me.

Not too bad.

At least I looked like a woman.

I went into the hall and waited for Hanna. She came out looking exactly like me. We shared the same green eyes, but I envied her honey-blonde hair.

"Ready?" I asked.

"Let's go!"

We met Miriam in the main hall.

"Well, don't you two look pretty," she said with her sweet smile.

I smiled and looked down.

"Thank you," Hanna said.

"Follow me, girls. Sadly, I have to split you two up." She looked at Hanna. "What is your name?"

"Hanna, ma'am."

"Hanna, you will tackle cleaning up the kitchen with these ladies." She looked at me. "And your name?"

"Ellena, ma'am."

"Ellena, you will come with me and tidy up the dining area."

Miriam was right about needing my hair up. The castle looked big from the outside but even bigger on the inside when I was cleaning it. I would have to thank her later.

At the end of the day, all of us servants were in the kitchen, seated around an enormous island, eating dinner.

"So, there is this really cute guard in the main hall. I caught him looking at me," Hanna gushed.

I shook my head, grinning.

"Did you notice any cute guys today?"

"I didn't. I was too busy *cleaning*." I looked at her playfully.

"Well, you missed out," she said, grinning and looking away.

I glanced around the island. Everyone appeared content. I knew it was my first day, but it seemed to me that the king and queen took care of their lowly servants.

I put my dishes in the sink and found Miriam. "Am I allowed to be in the gardens?" I had always loved being outside.

"Absolutely, dear! Just go out the kitchen, turn left, and it is right out the glass double doors on the left."

"Thank you."

I followed her instructions and found myself on the steps leading to the garden. It was beautiful. The walls surrounding the garden were draped in white string lights, illuminating the garden in a soft glow. It was a simple maze of bushes with trees dotted throughout. There was a fountain nestled in the back right corner. I decided to head there.

I made it to the fountain and saw that it was lit up by a soft blue light along the inside of the lip on the bottom. I could feel a light mist rolling out of it onto me.

"Beautiful," I whispered to myself.

"Isn't it?"

I jumped and turned to my right, where the voice had come from. A man sat on a bench, looking at me.

"I am so sorry! I didn't realize someone was here!" It was dark outside, and the string lights were behind him, so I could not make out his face.

"It's all right. I am not used to being invisible. It's kind of nice."

Odd thing to say. Maybe he has an important role in the castle.

Even though I wanted to stay and enjoy the garden, he was there first, and I didn't want to interrupt.

"I will let you get back to enjoying the evening. Good night."

He went to protest as I turned around. My foot caught on something, and down I went. I landed facedown on the grass. The stranger was at my side in a second, helping me up. Thank heavens it was dark outside because I could feel my face going bright red. I wiggled out of his grasp once I regained my footing.

"Thank you," I said, not looking at his face. I quickly walked back to the castle.

I sped all the way to my room, where I fell facedown on the bed. "Oh my gosh. Oh my gosh. Oh my gosh. What was that?" I replayed that awkward moment over and over. Needless to say, I did not sleep well.

Hanna laughed as I recalled the whole thing to her at breakfast.

"Shut up, Han!"

"You would be laughing too if it happened to me."

I nodded my head in agreement, bashfully.

"Was he cute?"

I smacked her.

"Ellena, there is a spill on the dining table. Could you get it please?" Miriam asked.

"Of course, ma'am."

"Now, the prince is still eating, so try to be in and out quickly."

Hanna looked at me with jealousy in her eyes. "Lucky!"

I just rolled my eyes, grinned, and got up.

I kept my head down as I entered and got busy cleaning up the spilled cup. Even though I was not as boy crazy as Hanna, I was still excited to be in the same room as the prince. I dared a peek at him.

My eyes went wide. There, sitting with his fork paused by his mouth, staring at me, was the man from last night.

CHAPTER 2

HE BROKE INTO A GRIN. "HELLO AGAIN."

I felt my face go red. "Hello," I stammered.

You have got to be kidding me! The prince is the one I made a fool of myself in front of?

No wonder he thought it was so nice to be invisible.

"You weren't supposed to be home until today," I said in shock, my eyes still wide.

He ran his hand through his hair. "Yeah. We came to an agreement faster than I anticipated."

"That's good." I started to relax a little bit.

"It is," he said with a smile.

A butler came in and whispered something in his ear.

He nodded his head. "Thank you." He looked back to me. "I am sorry, miss, but I am needed. I hope to see you around?"

All I could do was nod my head a couple of times.

He left.

I finished cleaning up the mess and headed back toward the kitchen.

I only got one foot through the doorway when Hanna grabbed my arm and dragged me to the side.

"How is he?" she asked excitedly.

"He is, indeed, very handsome. And kind."

"I knew it!"

"And … the guy from last night."

She froze. "Are you serious!" She tried to hide the smile creeping in.

"Dead serious."

"Oh, Ellena, I am so sorry." She started to giggle.

"Butthead," I said, smiling, walking away.

Miriam asked me to tackle sweeping and mopping the two outside stairs before it got too hot outside.

They were beautiful, polished marble. I imagined heels clicking across them. I imagined *me* in those heels, in a beautiful gown, being welcomed into the castle. My thoughts were cut short by a cold voice.

"Daydreaming, are we?"

I looked to the door and saw Hugo, arms crossed, with a smirk across his face.

"Sorry, sir." I looked down and got back to work. I could feel him still staring at me. I returned my eyes to him.

"Can I help you, sir?"

He shook his head. "Not today." He turned and walked away.

What the heck?

I finished up my morning chores and went into the kitchen for lunch. I saw Hanna flirting with one of the other staff members. They were both enjoying it. I envied not only her beautiful hair but also her confidence and skill at wrapping any man around her finger in an instant.

I sat down by myself. The food was incredible. Even as a servant, I was indulging in the crispiest fried fish and potatoes and the freshest lemonade I'd ever had.

My lunch was over all too soon, and I had to get back to work.

"I need you to dust the library. It will take the rest of the day," Miriam said.

I paused. "Did you say library?" I felt a smile appear.

She cocked an eyebrow at me. "I did." She smiled. "Dust first, read later."

"Yes, ma'am."

The double doors to the library were already open when I approached. I stood in the doorway in awe.

Directly in front was a wall that was one giant window. It lit up the library wonderfully. In the middle of the room was a large, rectangular area rug, with a couple of leather couches and armchairs placed around it. The two walls on the sides were floor to ceiling, covered in shelves that were filled with books. They were broken into two levels, with metal spiral staircases leading to the second floor and matching metal railings.

I knew it might have been a chore for others, but for me, it was heaven.

I ran the duster along each shelf, looking at titles as I went by. It appeared that anything a leader of the country would need—political science, history, nonfiction—was located on the lower level. It made sense. It made them more easily accessible. My favorites—fiction, fantasy, romance—were all located on the top levels. Miriam was right; dusting the library kept me busy the rest of the day. I did not even go to dinner. I was not hungry, and it helped me finish sooner so that I could get to reading.

It was dark outside, and the chandelier in the center of the library came on. It had strings of diamonds draped below the bulbs. It gave a sparkly glow to the room.

I glanced through the romances first. After the third cover that made me blush, I decided to abandon those. I found a fantasy and got nestled into one of the armchairs. I read on into the night, and at some point, I fell asleep.

I woke to light rustling nearby. I slowly opened my eyes and saw the prince seated in the opposite armchair, sipping coffee and reading a newspaper. I sat up with a start. He looked up.

"Did you sleep well?"

I felt myself turning red. "Yes, Your Highness."

He smiled, got up, and picked up the book that had fallen to the floor. "Do you like it?"

"I did," I replied, avoiding his gaze.

"Did? You finished it all in one night?"

"Yes, Your Highness." I looked up at him.

He curled his lips. "Impressive."

"Thank you, Your Highness."

He handed me the book and went back to his chair. "So, you're a fan of fiction?"

I nodded my head, smiling. "Yes, Your Highness."

"Please, call me Jonathon."

I nodded with a smile again. "Okay."

"If you liked that book," he said, getting up and motioning for me to follow him, "then you will like these." He led us up to the second floor and showed me a series of half a dozen books.

"Fair warning, it will take longer than one night to read them," he said with a smile.

I looked up at him, smiling. "We'll see."

He chuckled.

He was so handsome. He had thick, chestnut-brown hair with a slight wave to it and brown eyes that reminded me of milk chocolate. He had the same rectangular face as his father. Feeling embarrassed that I looked as long as I did, I looked back to the books.

"You are welcome to read in here anytime you like."

"Thank you. I would like that very much—*after* I finish my duties first." I smiled.

"Of course."

"Speaking of which, I should probably get started on those." I started to walk away.

"Hold on. I didn't catch your name."

"Ellena."

"Ellena," he repeated with a smile and slight bow.

I gave a small curtsy and headed out of there before he could catch my blush.

"Dear heavens, child! Where have you been?" Miriam asked.

"I'm sorry. I fell asleep in the library." I looked down.

She sighed. "It's okay, dear. You still beat your friend here."

I giggled and shook my head. *Oh, Hanna.*

"I am going to need you to vacuum all of the carpeted areas on this floor."

"Yes, ma'am."

I headed to the supply closet. The vacuum was deep inside. I grabbed it and went to head out when my exit was blocked by someone. Hugo.

His cold eyes were on mine.

"We have not properly met. I am Hugo." He held out his hand.

Reluctantly, I put my hand in his. "Ellena."

"Beautiful name," he said as he stroked my knuckles. I quickly withdrew my hand.

He smirked.

"If you would please, I have things to do." I nodded at the door.

He stayed put for a few more seconds, staring at me, then moved to the side, allowing just enough room for me to get by but not enough without having to brush past him. I felt a chill crawl up my back.

Since I had skipped dinner and breakfast, I was starving by lunch. I grabbed my food and joined Hanna, who was waving wildly to me.

We smiled and hugged.

"It has been forever since we have talked!"

"Han, it's been a day."

"Like I said, *forever*!"

I shook my head, smiling.

"What have they been having you do?"

"Yesterday, I dusted the library. Today, I am vacuuming the whole first floor. You?"

"I have been washing windows," she said, sticking a finger in her throat.

We laughed.

I could not resist. "Any cute boys?"

She beamed. "Tons! I feel like I am in eye-candy-land! Sadly, I have yet to see the prince." She looked at me jealously.

"It's no big deal. All three times were very short conversations."

Uh-oh.

She sat up straight. "*Three* times? When was the other time?"

I told her all about the library.

She leaned her head onto her fist. "I think he likes you."

"He is kind. That's all."

She shook her head.

"Okay, let's entertain your *crazy* idea. I am a nobody. Just one of the many people employed by his parents." I could tell by her goofy smile she was not being swayed.

"I am going back to work," I said.

At the end of the day, I headed to the library, picked out the first book in the series that the prince—sorry, *Jonathon*—recommended, and nestled into what was quickly becoming *my* armchair.

Surprisingly, I stopped halfway through and went to bed. I did not want *another* embarrassing situation with Jonathon again.

CHAPTER 3

SO MUCH FOR THAT. A COUPLE OF DAYS WENT BY without incident. That was probably because I did not see him for a couple of days. You know that old phrase, third time's a charm? I guess that does not apply when you had charm the first two times.

The next day, I was at the end of the hallway by the library, watering the ficus tree that stood in front of the window. Some water splashed out and over the side of the pot onto the wall.

Crap.

I put the watering can down, grabbed my apron, and started to wipe up my mess.

"Hello there," a voice greeted.

Startled, I stood up quickly, right into the branches of the ficus tree, knocking it over.

"Whoa!" the person exclaimed, catching the tree before it crashed to the floor.

"Oh my gosh! I am so sorry!" I said as I grabbed the tree from no other than the prince.

You have got to be kidding me!

"It is all right! I am so sorry to have startled you." He looked down to the spot where I had been. "What were you doing down there anyway?" He raised an eyebrow at me.

"I spilled some water on the wall and was cleaning it up," I answered, putting the tree back where it belonged.

"Ahhh." A smirk crept over his face.

We stood in awkward silence for a minute.

"Well, I should probably get back to watering the plants."

"You're right. I will leave you to it then." He gave a small bow, and I curtsied.

After he disappeared down the hall, I leaned back against the window and put my hands over my face.

Oh my gosh! How humiliating!

I took a deep breath, lowered my hands, and turned to the tree.

"Freaking ficus," I grumbled as I picked up the watering can and got back to my duties.

I avoided him like the plague for the next few days, not walking by the dining room around mealtimes and ducking into rooms when I saw him in the same hallway. Hanna caught me one time.

"What in the world are you doing?" she asked.

I peeked around the wall to make sure he was gone. I recounted the story about the ficus. She burst out laughing.

"Shh!" I demanded, looking around.

"Oh, Ellena, I am so sorry, but that is too funny!" She was hunched over, holding onto her stomach.

I crossed my arms and waited for her to finish laughing.

She stood up and wiped the tears from her eyes.

"Are you done?"

"Yeah." She still had a huge smile plastered on her face.

"Why does this keep happening? I can't stop embarrassing myself in front of him!"

She gave me a sympathetic shrug.

I sighed.

"We should probably get back to work," I said, and we made our way down the hall.

I did not try to actively avoid him anymore. I did not want anyone else catching me like that again, *especially* him.

I was heading to my usual spot in the library at the end of another long day. It had been a couple of days since I finished the series Jonathon showed me, so I was onto a new one.

I had only been there for about an hour when Jonathon walked in, looking very tired. His hair was a mess, and he had his suit coat off, with the shirt sleeves rolled up to just below his elbows. That was the first time I got to get a peek at his physique. I could tell he was muscular. I could not help but wonder how he looked without a shirt.

Stop that.

Our eyes met, and we smiled at the same time. He headed over and collapsed into the other armchair.

"You okay?" I asked.

Even though he was tired, he still had a warm sparkle to his eyes. "Yeah. Just had some issues come up that needed immediate addressing."

"Were you able to get them resolved?"

"For now."

"That's good," I said, looking down into my lap.

I was so shy. Why could I not be more like Hanna? I bet he found me so awkward to be around.

"It's been a while. How are you doing with that series?"

I shook the book in my hand. "I finished it and am onto another one."

He smiled. "I should've known."

I smiled, looking down again.

"You know, I'm starving. Would you like to join me in the kitchen for a late-night snack?"

I looked up and froze.

Get your bearings, girl.

I smiled. "I'd like that."

I sat down at the empty island. He brought over a glass of wine with some cheese and crackers. We ate and drank in silence for a few minutes.

"So, which orphanage did you come from?"

"Madam Greer's."

"I hear she is an *interesting* individual."

"That's one way to put it." I grinned.

We enjoyed the food some more.

"Do you like it here?" he asked.

"Very much. I didn't think I would feel so comfortable here. And the food is fantastic," I said, putting another piece of cheese into my mouth.

He chuckled. "The chefs are pretty incredible."

There was a pause.

"This might be a silly question. Do you like it here?" I asked.

He pondered before answering. "More often than not, yes. I love helping the people of Olandia and being surrounded by such comforts. But sometimes I wish I could be invisible—not bothered for a day, you know?"

"I can only imagine. You guys do a wonderful job, just so you know. Taking care of the people."

He smiled. "Thank you. We try."

Shortly thereafter, we finished our snack.

"May I escort you back to your room?"

I was surprised. "Really?"

He laughed. "Is that all right?"

"It is," I said, smiling. I could tell it was huge.

The walk back was over far too soon.

"Thank you for including me with your late-night snack. I really enjoyed it."

"You are most welcome. You were very pleasurable company." He gave a slight bow, and I replied with a curtsy.

I went into my room. My knees gave out, and I fell onto my bed. I could not stop myself from smiling like an idiot until I fell asleep.

I woke to Miriam knocking on my door. "Meet in the main hall first this morning. The family has an announcement."

I got dressed, threw my hair into a messy bun, and walked with Hanna to the main hall. Every servant was there. The king, queen, and Jonathon were all up front on their little stage.

"Good morning, everyone!" King Olov greeted. "My niece, Lisette, is coming to visit! She will be here this afternoon. I am needing someone to be her maid during her stay. Miriam, is there anyone you recommend?"

"Yes, sire. I believe Ellena is up for the task." She motioned for me to step forward. I gave a curtsy to the royal family.

"Wonderful! Also, during her stay, I am wanting to throw a ball!"

There were gasps, giggles, and clapping from everyone.

"It will be in one week's time. So, things are going to be a little more crazy around here, but I know we can all pull off a spectacular party. Thank you all for coming. Miriam? Ellena? Please come up."

I followed his directions, feeling my heart skip a beat as I felt Jonathon's eyes on me.

"Miriam, would you please get her into the maid's uniform and then have her report back here when she is ready?"

"Absolutely, Your Majesty."

We both curtsied, and I followed her to the basement, where she went into a closet and pulled out a new outfit for me. I went to my room and put it on. It was a much more form-fitting white, three-quarter-sleeve shirt, with a thick-strapped black dress that went to mid-calf.

The royal family, a couple of guards, and I were outside the front doors when Lisette's carriage pulled up.

She was gorgeous. She was young and had light blonde hair that fell a little past her shoulders, done in curls. Her porcelain skin glowed, and she had the prettiest smile.

"Lisette!" the king greeted as she ran into his arms.

"Uncle! Aunt Leona! Jonathon!" she exclaimed as she went down the line, hugging each one.

"This is your maid, Ellena. She will take your things for you." The king motioned to me.

I curtsied. She did the same. I gathered her belongings and followed her to the room that one of the guards led her to on the third floor.

"You can put those down over there please." She pointed to the corner.

I put her bags down.

"How long have you been here?"

"Almost two weeks, ma'am."

"And you haven't run for the hills yet?"

I chuckled. "No, ma'am."

"Well, you are going to be with me for the next week. That just might change." She winked at me.

I smiled. "I highly doubt that, ma'am."

"Why is that?"

"I have yet to come across a mean Larsson. You seem just as nice as the rest of them."

She nodded, grinning widely.

After getting Lisette ready for dinner, we walked down to the dining room. The men stood as she entered. However, Jonathon did not look at her but me. I looked down, hiding my blush, and took my place behind her along the wall. They sat back down.

I loved watching them all. They got along so well. Even though they were more relaxed in here, they still had an air of humble power around them.

"How is your maid treating you?" the king asked.

I felt all eyes on me, and my eyes went wide.

"I like her very much," she said, turning around and smiling at me.

I smiled back and saw behind her that Jonathon was smiling too. My heart skipped.

We made eye contact a few more times throughout dinner, nearly leaving me breathless each time.

I shut her suite door after we entered.

"So, what did you do to catch my cousin's eye?" she asked, sitting down at her vanity.

I whirled around, blushing furiously. "Excuse me, ma'am?"

"You heard me," she insisted, smiling with her arms folded.

I looked down. "I don't believe I am anyone special. He is just very kind is all."

"Tsk, tsk, tsk. I have never seen him look at a girl like that before."

I could feel my face darken to a deeper shade of red.

She giggled. "You like him too, don't you!"

I shrugged. "Not that anything will come of it. He is a prince, and I am just a servant in his home."

"Pfft, like that means anything nowadays. This is the twenty-first century, dear."

We grinned at each other. She turned back to the vanity and proceeded to take off her jewelry.

After she finished there, I helped her change into her nightgown.

"Is there anything else I can do for you, ma'am?" I asked.

"No, thank you. You may go."

CHAPTER 4

AFTER LEAVING LISETTE'S ROOM THE NEXT NIGHT, I headed to the library like usual. While I was searching for a new book, there was a flash of light, followed by a crack that shook the room. I looked out the windows. Rain began to patter against the glass.

I loved rainstorms, the way the world quieted and how it washed everything away. I loved the smell when everything got wet. I loved the feel of the rain on my skin.

Another bright flash followed by a deafening boom knocked the power out.

There are exceptions to everything, like right then. I *hated* when a storm knocked the power out at night. I hated the dark.

I slid down the bookshelf until I was on the floor. I curled my legs against my chest, wrapped my arms around them, and rested my head in the middle.

Please someone find me in here.

My plea was answered a few minutes later when someone entered the library with an oil lamp in hand.

"Ellena?" a familiar voice asked.

Jonathon.

"I am up here," I responded tapping the bookshelf above me. He was up the stairs and beside me in no time.

"How did you know I was here?" I asked.

"I checked your room first, to see if you had made it back before the power went out. When I saw you were not there, I remembered how much you like to read. So … here I am," he said, smiling.

I felt my heartbeat pick up. "That is really sweet of you … to check up on me."

He looked down, still smiling, and started fiddling with the lamp.

Another flash and crack filled the room.

I involuntarily leaned into him.

I pulled back. "I am sorry."

He put his arm around me and pulled me back to him.

"Afraid of storms, huh?"

"Not usually. Only when the power goes out. I may be an adult, but I still hate the dark."

I expected him to laugh at my admission, but he did not.

"The dark makes a lot of people uneasy." He rubbed my arm.

"Are you afraid of the dark?"

"Only if I do not have a light with me."

I do not know how long we sat there, but it must have been a while because the next thing I knew, he was waking me up.

"Ellena? The power is back on," he whispered. I opened my eyes and saw I was on his chest. I slowly sat up and stretched.

"Would you like me to take you back to your room?"

I nodded sleepily.

He stood and helped me up. We walked down the library staircase. I missed the last step. Luckily, he caught me before I landed face-first this time.

I looked up at him, snorted, then started laughing.

"That was almost really bad," I said, half out of it.

He chuckled. "You are too tired to walk." He put the lamp down and picked me up.

He carried me like I was nothing, back to my room.

He opened the door, walked over, and placed me into my bed.

"Thank you," I whispered, and I drifted off again.

I could not stop smiling as I got ready the next morning. I was dumbfounded that Jonathon, a prince, had taken an interest in me. I silently squealed and jumped up and down.

However, could anything ever come of it? He was a prince. I was an orphan, a housekeeper turned maid, a nobody. I appreciated Hanna and Lisette's hopeful words, but Hanna was a hopeless romantic; maybe Lisette was too. My heart started to hurt, and my giddiness faded.

I started to head to Lisette's room.

You know what? Who cares?

So what if nothing was going to come of us. I have never been looked at by a man the way that Jonathon did; never felt my heart do the things that it does when he is around. I am going to let myself enjoy every last minute of his attention, even if it does come to an eventual end.

I was disappointed that, for the next couple of days, I only saw Jonathon at mealtimes. Do not get me wrong. There were many glances and hidden smiles, but my heart ached for another conversation with him, another touch.

My heart started to race when I felt eyes on me in the library that night. However, upon looking up, my heart sank into my stomach. It was not Jonathon but Hugo. He was slowly, *very slowly*, walking past the library, staring at me. I stared back, grimacing. This brought a smirk to his face as he disappeared past the wall.

I had not talked to Hanna since becoming Lisette's maid; just smiles as we saw each other around the castle. I was finally able to hang out with her the night before the ball in her room and catch her up on everything having to do with Jonathon.

She squealed.

"Shh! Others will hear you."

"So? Let them hear! The prince has eyes for you-who."

I rolled my eyes, grinning. "How is it going with you in the boy department?"

She grinned. "I have kissed a couple."

"No way!"

"Yes way! They initiated them, so ..." She blushed.

"That is great, Han," I said, smiling.

We talked through the night until we fell asleep on her bed.

I was pulling Lisette's hair back into a braid for breakfast when she asked, "Would you like to go to the ball with me as my guest?"

I stopped and looked at her through the mirror. "You can't be serious."

"Why wouldn't I be? I think you deserve a night off, and I think Jonathon would love to see you all done up."

I blushed and finished her braid.

"Am I allowed?" I asked.

"Of course, you are! I am their guest, and this is a request of mine."

Holy crap.

I felt a huge smile spread across my face.

"I would love that."

"Yay!" she sang, clapping her hands. "After dinner, we will take turns getting each other all done up!"

The day dragged on. I could not wait until the ball that night. I kept imagining different outfits and hairstyles on me, along with Jonathon's expression when he would first see me.

I was able to tell Hanna the exciting news at lunch. She squealed so loudly that the others looked our direction. I stared at her, nodding to the audience she attracted.

"Oh, I don't care! You are going to a ball!"

I buried my face in my hands.

"What?" Miriam asked, walking over excitedly.

"Lisette has made Ellena her guest at the ball tonight!"

She squealed louder than Hanna.

"That is so exciting! I can't wait to see you! What dress are you wearing?"

"I don't know yet!"

"How are you doing your hair?"

"I don't know! Lisette is going to be making me over. I will be just as surprised as you guys."

Miriam was ecstatic.

"Watch for us from the kitchen!"

"Okay!" I smiled.

The waiting *finally* came to an end with dinner. Lisette and I rushed to her room. It seemed she was just as excited as I was.

I got her ready first.

She put on a silky green dress with straps that hung off her shoulders and was low-cut on the front and back. It hugged her womanly curves and went down to the floor. She requested that I part her hair on the side and curl it all, leaving it down. She was beautiful.

Then it was my turn. Thankfully, we were similar in size. I put on her selected dress.

It was a deep, midnight blue. The opaque fabric was a strapless that went down to my knees, but a sheer material covered up to my neck, down my arms to my wrists, and laid over the rest of the dress. The sheer material was covered in little, sparkling diamonds. She gave me a pair of matching blue heels that had to be two inches high.

How the heck am I supposed to dance in these?

I sat down at the vanity, and she started on my hair.

She parted it on one side and put it into a braid that went over the opposite shoulder. She curled the hairs around my face that never wanted to stay in. She gave me dangling diamond earrings that matched the dress. Lastly, she addressed my makeup.

"Now, you are a natural beauty. So, all I am going to do is enhance what you already have." She proceeded to put on a tinted moisturizer, mascara, and a light brown lipstick.

I went and stood in front of the full-length mirror. I looked like I belonged in the night sky.

"How do you feel?" she asked.

"Beautiful," I replied as I turned around and hugged her. She wrapped her arms around me too.

"My cousin will not be able to keep his eyes off you. Let's go."

I blushed as I put my arm through hers and we made our way out into the hall.

My stomach was doing flips as we headed to the stairs that would take us to the main hall. I stopped just short of the stairs.

"I can't do this," I said looking at her.

She took my hands in hers. "Yes, you can. You are going to be the most beautiful girl in there. Well, next to me, of course." She winked.

I laughed.

"Now, I am going down first, so you have your own entrance."

What?

"He usually socializes for a bit before joining in the festivities, so he will most likely be along the sides. I will make sure he is by and facing the stairs. Give me five minutes."

She let go of my hands and proceeded down the stairs.

I felt like throwing up. My hands were getting sweaty.

You can do this. You can do this.

After counting to three hundred, I took a deep breath and headed down the stairs.

At first, I kept my head down, making sure I did not trip down the stairs in the freaking heels. I could hear Jonathon talking to someone. Then he stopped. I felt eyes on me. I looked up. There he was, looking absolutely dashing in his black suit, with a single middle button done, no tie, and the top button of his shirt undone. He was looking at me, mouth slightly agape. I could see Lisette next to him. Without looking at her, I knew she was grinning ear to ear. He started walking toward me. I finally reached the floor.

Thank God.

He smiled, his eyes twinkling. "You look incredible," he said, offering me his arm.

I took it, hoping he did not notice the tremble in my arm.

I smiled. "Thank you."

He led me out to the dance floor. I could feel other eyes turning to me, but I could not take my eyes off his.

As if he could sense my fear, he whispered, "Deep breaths. Keep looking at me. You're doing fine." He smiled. I smiled nervously back.

We finally made it to an open spot where he stopped and brought me out in front, facing him. He put one arm around my waist and held up the other.

Oh crap.

My eyes went wide. "I don't know how to dance," I whispered.

How the heck did we skip that *preparation step?*

I looked around him and at Lisette, my eyes still wide. She mouthed, "I am so sorry!"

He let out a low chuckle. "It's okay. Just follow my lead. I will stick to simple moves."

I nodded and nervously put my hand in his. He pulled me in close. I put my other arm on his shoulder.

He whispered, "Right foot, back." I followed. "Left foot, left. Bring the right to the left. Left foot, forward. Right foot, forward and sideways. Bring the left to the right. Good," he instructed, smiling. I grinned.

We settled into a nice rhythm for a few minutes.

An evil grin settled on his face.

I looked at him, cocking an eyebrow. "What?"

"Let's travel."

"What?"

He tightened his grip on me and then started traveling around the room. I pressed up against him. It was exhilarating. I started to laugh.

We came toward the hall by the kitchen, where half a dozen heads poked out from behind the wall. Miriam and Hanna waved enthusiastically. I lifted my hand off his shoulder and waved back, smiling. He turned to see who I was waving to.

"Friends of yours?" he asked, smiling at them.

"Yes."

"I know Miriam. Who is the girl next to her?"

"My best friend, Hanna. We grew up in the orphanage together."

He turned his attention back to me. "I'm glad you guys were able to stay together."

"Me too."

We stopped traveling but continued with the movements for a minute longer.

"The song is winding down. May I spin you?"

I swallowed. "Sure."

He spun me out, my dress spreading out around me. I felt like a princess. He spun me back in, but kept it going an extra spin so that my back was against his arm, and he dipped me. His face was hovering above mine. There could have only been a couple of inches between us. We stayed like that for a moment.

"Will you accompany me to the gardens?" he whispered.

"Absolutely."

He let me up, held out his arm, and I grabbed onto it.

When we made it out onto the stairs overlooking the gardens, I pulled on his arm and asked, "Do you mind if I take these things off?" shaking my foot.

He laughed. "Of course."

I held onto his arm while I took the shoes off.

"Better?"

"Much."

We descended the stairs, and my bare feet hit the grass. I could not help but close my eyes and soak in the feel. I opened my eyes to see him watching me.

"Sorry. I love the feel of grass on my feet."

"No need to be sorry," he said, smiling.

We turned left and looked like we were going to be taking the path around the whole garden. I felt giddy thinking about him taking the long way around with me. We walked in silence along the first side. We turned and followed the path along the back wall.

"Are you enjoying yourself this evening?" he asked.

I smiled. "I am. Are you?"

"Very much so." He brought his other hand up to lay on my hand that was holding onto his arm. My heart skipped a beat. We soon came to the fountain in the corner.

I let out a low groan.

"What is it?" He saw me looking ahead at the fountain.

He laughed. "That was funny."

I looked at him. "It was mortifying!" I could not help but laugh too.

He brought us to the bench, and we both sat down. We stared at the water cascading down the fountain for a few minutes. I was so nervous about what I wanted to say next, but I felt like he more than deserved it.

I looked down and cleared my throat. "I don't think I have told you yet tonight, but you look really good in that suit." I peeked at him.

He turned and looked at me, smiling slightly. "Thank you."

I nodded.

"I know I already told you, but you look incredible tonight. You look like you belong in the night sky."

I put my hand on his arm and sat up excitedly. "That's exactly what I thought earlier!" I said, smiling.

I looked down at my hand on his arm and went to move it. He quickly placed his hand on top of it.

My breath flew right out of me. He started to rub my knuckles slowly. No matter how hard I tried, I could not get my breath back. I looked up at him. He was looking at me. My eyes took turns looking between each of his eyes. He started to move his face closer to mine. My eyes now looked from his eyes to his lips. He was so close now. I could feel his breath on my face. I closed my eyes, and our lips touched.

I felt an overwhelming tingle start on my lips, go across my face, over my head, down my spine, and out to my extremities. He pulled away.

I grabbed what little bit of air I could and planted my own lips on his this time. One of his hands wrapped around my waist, while the other went up to my neck. I placed one hand on his muscular chest, and the other held the side of his face.

Our lips glided over each other's smoothly. His lips were so soft. He parted his lips ever so slightly, and I did the same. We pulled away, each of us a little out of breath. We stared into each other's face, smiling.

Bang! An unmistakable shot rang through the air. He instinctively pushed me to the ground and covered my body with his.

Chaos erupted around us.

"I need to go find Hanna!" I shouted.

"No, you're not! You are not going in there!"

"You need to help your family! I need to help my friends! I know about the safe rooms. I will get us to one."

I could see him struggling.

"Okay." He helped me to my feet. "Just to the kitchen, then to the safe room."

I nodded. We both took off running back to the castle.

Another shot echoed through the air as he disappeared into the frantic crowd inside.

"Please, God, keep him safe."

I turned into the kitchen and found Hanna, Miriam, and a couple of other servants crouched behind the island.

"Come! We need to get to the safe room!" I grabbed Hanna's hand. The others followed. We zigzagged to the end of the hall, running as fast as we could. I ran my hands along the wall until I found the switch to open the wall.

"Go!" I pushed Hanna in, then Miriam, then the others. I quickly followed and shut the door, deadbolting it. I found the switch and turned on the light.

We all jumped as a couple more shots rang out. I collapsed along the wall by Hanna and took her in my right arm. I brought my knees to my chest and clutched them with my left.

Please, God, keep him safe.

CHAPTER 5

I DO NOT KNOW HOW LONG WE WERE IN THERE. IT seemed like an eternity though, worrying about the safety of those around me.

Jonathon. I hoped he was okay.

A knock came at the door. Miriam pressed her ear to it and asked for the password. She must have heard it because the next thing she did was undo the deadbolt and open the door.

A guard was on the other side. "Is everyone okay? Any injuries?"

We all looked at ourselves and one another and shook our heads.

"Good. The king and queen have asked that housekeeping help with the cleanup but that everyone else go to their rooms."

I helped Hanna to her feet. We followed Miriam until she gave us assignments, then got busy cleaning up.

The main hall was a mess. A couple of windows were broken, and there were broken wine glasses scattered around the floor. I looked for any sign of Jonathon. The guard mentioned the king and queen, so I knew they had made it, but what about him?

I shook the terrifying thought away.

After sweeping up all the glass, Hanna and I checked with Miriam, who told us to head back to our rooms.

I tucked Hanna into her bed and then crossed the hall to my room and went in.

I looked at myself in the mirror. The dress was dirty, my hair was falling out, and my makeup was smeared. I changed into pajamas, brushed out my hair, and wiped off the smeared makeup. I heard a knock at my door.

Please.

I opened it slowly at first, then threw it open and jumped into his arms when I saw it was Jonathon. He held me tight and kissed my forehead.

"Oh, thank God," he said, full of relief.

"I was so worried," I stammered.

He put me down, grabbed my face, and planted a heated kiss on my lips. After he pulled away, I put my hands on his, and we stared at each other. My knees were going weak as he stroked my cheeks. Tears were welling up in my eyes.

"Shh," he whispered as he kissed my forehead again and pulled me into his chest. I wrapped my arms around his abdomen.

"Who was that? What did they want?"

"I don't know if I should be sharing this, but it's a group that is displeased with my father. They had only been sending threatening letters … until tonight."

"What are they so upset about?"

"We are not sure yet. All we know is that they are displeased with how he runs the country. They have been very vague so far."

"Hm."

We stood there, holding each other for a few more minutes.

"I am so sorry, but I need to meet with my parents. There is much we have to discuss. I just had to come by and see that you were safe first."

We squeezed each other one last time before he turned and went up the stairs.

I went back into my room and crawled into bed. It did not take me long to fall asleep.

I was woken up by someone knocking on my door. It was Miriam.

"Good morning, ma'am," I greeted.

"Good morning, Ellena. Your presence is requested in the main hall. The king and queen want to speak with you."

My eyes grew wide. "What on earth for?"

"I have no idea. I will accompany you."

"Let me change. I will be out in a few minutes."

I shut the door, threw on my maid outfit, and pulled my hair back into a ponytail.

"Let's go!" I said to Miriam as I opened and shut my door.

What in the world do they want to meet with me for?

What if they were displeased with me behaving like someone above their station last night?

Crap.

My nervousness went through the roof when I saw Jonathon beside his mother and father.

Great. I am going to get yelled at in front of him.

He was smiling.

Maybe things are going to be okay.

I curtsied to the royal family. "Your Majesties."

The king and queen both smiled at me.

"Ellena," the king started, "because of your act of bravery last night, we are promoting you to the status of lady. You will now reside on the third floor with our other guests."

My eyes went wide, and I looked between all three of them.

Are you serious?

"Are you okay, Lady Ellena?" the queen asked.

I shook my head. "I am so sorry, Your Majesty. I am in shock."

I let out a quiet sigh. "I am humbled by your kind gesture and accept it gratefully," I said as I curtsied.

"Excellent," the king said, smiling. "Miriam will help you get set up in your new room."

"Thank you." I gave a final curtsy and turned to follow Miriam.

My jaw dropped as Miriam opened the door to my suite. It had a set of double doors along the back wall. I ran over to them and flung them open.

"I have my own balcony!" I quietly squealed.

I inhaled a breath of fresh air.

I turned around and looked at the rest of my room. I had a bathroom in the left corner, a closet in the right corner, a gold vanity next to the closet, a small table with two chairs by the bedroom doors, and a massive bed in the middle of the left wall with a nightstand next to it.

I could not help myself. I ran over to the bed and jumped onto it, lying sprawled out on it as if I were making a snow angel.

"I can't believe it," I said, staring at the ceiling.

"You have earned it, miss," Miriam said, smiling.

I sat up. "I simply did what I believe any sensible person would do."

"That's the thing, miss. Not everyone is sensible. That is what makes it extraordinary."

There was a knock at the door. Miriam opened it, and Lisette stepped in.

"Ha-ha! Look at you!" She wrapped me in a hug.

"Thank you again for last night. It was incredible … except for that last part."

We were all silent for a moment.

"I am glad to see that you are okay," I continued.

"Yeah, a rather cute guard got me to a safe room," she said, smiling. "And you are welcome."

"Is there anything else I can do for you, Ellena?" Miriam inquired.

"No, thank you. You may go."

After Miriam shut the door behind her, Lisette turned to me excitedly. "You cannot be a lady in the clothes you have. No offense."

I raised an eyebrow.

None taken ...

"I'm taking you shopping!"

The car came to a stop in front of Belle's Boutique, a place I had walked by many times but knew I could never afford to go into. We walked in.

The place was full of dresses. There was a section for casual dresses, short party dresses, long evening wear, and more. Lisette led me to the long dresses first.

"What tickles your fancy?"

I looked through the rack of clothes. They were all so over-the-top fancy that I was about to give up when a style caught my eye. The dress had spaghetti straps. The breast area was ruched, with an empire waist. The rest of the dress went straight to the floor.

I turned to Lisette, holding up the dress. "This one."

"Which color?"

I had not realized there was more than one color. I was holding a sky-blue one. There was also a plum, forest green, satin red, and black. I flipped between all of them multiple times.

"One of each then!" Lisette said, grabbing each of the dresses.

Before I could protest, she led me to the next section.

Despite my best efforts to keep my dresses simple, she refused to let me walk out of the store without at least three fancy ones.

"Thank you so much," I said on the ride back to the castle, holding my bags of dresses. "You really shouldn't have."

"Oh hush. It's not every day I get to turn a maid into a princess!"

"I am not a princess."

"You will be someday." She winked.

I shook my head, grinning, and watched the scenery pass across the window the rest of the way back.

Lisette helped me carry my bags to my room. "I can't wait to see what you wear to dinner!"

"I attend those as a guest now?"

"You sure do! And it is my last night, so you better make it good." She smiled and left.

I hung up all the dresses in my walk-in closet. I stared at the dangling, silky fabrics.

What in the world was I going to wear?

I decided on the black one so that it would not show any inevitable spills. I straightened, then pulled my hair back into a half ponytail. I only owned one pair of earrings, a set of silver posts. I put them on. Even though I knew I would not compare with Lisette, I felt pretty for my first dinner as a lady.

I took deep breaths the whole way down to the dining room. I could hear everyone inside already.

Great. Late for my first lady dinner.

I stepped into the room. The king stood up as he always did. Jonathon did too, but he was so abrupt that his chair made a scratching sound on the floor. He stared at me.

"Lady Ellena," he said, giving a slight bow, never breaking eye contact.

I returned with a small curtsy and a smile.

I was shown to the seat right next to Lisette and directly across from Jonathon.

I looked down at the place setting and felt my eyes go wide.

Jonathon cleared his throat. I looked up at him. He pointed to the utensil I should use first.

"Thank you," I mouthed.

With the help of Jonathon, dinner was incident-free. I stood up, and Jonathon did the same.

"I wondered if you wouldn't mind me escorting you back to your room?" he asked.

I smiled. "That would be wonderful, thank you."

I turned to the king and queen. "Thank you for a wonderful evening."

They nodded, smiling.

Jonathon came around the table and held out his arm for me. I threaded my arm through it. We started the walk back to the third floor very slowly. I did not mind one bit.

"You did great tonight."

"Ha! I merely survived, but thank you. And thank you for all of the help again."

"It was my pleasure."

We walked silently for a bit.

"You look beautiful tonight. I really like that dress."

I smiled and nervously tucked a loose hair behind my ear. "Thank you. I have four more just like it."

"I am looking forward to seeing them all."

We came up to my door. He turned to face me. He took my hands into his.

"Ellena …" He paused, taking a breath. "I was wondering …"

He paused again, looking down. I had never seen him nervous. It was adorable.

I tilted my head to the side so I could see his face.

"Yes?"

He looked up at me and took a deep breath. "I was wondering if you would join me in an official courtship?"

I cocked an eyebrow. "And that is royal for?"

"Will you do me the honor of becoming my girlfriend?"

I broke into a huge smile. "Of course I will."

He picked me up into his arms. "Thank you, Ellena."

He put me back down but kept his arms around my waist.

I looked into his eyes. "As if I could have answered any other way."

He leaned down and kissed me softly.

I pulled back. "What about your parents? Will they approve?"

He smiled. "I asked them this morning. They more than approve."

This time, I was the one to kiss him.

I will never get tired of kissing this man.

He pulled away. "Good night, Lady Ellena." He took my hand and lightly kissed my knuckles.

"Good night, Your Highness." I gave him a curtsy.

He watched me go into my room and shut the door. I pressed my ear to it until I could no longer hear his footsteps.

I went and fell onto my bed, face-first into a pillow, and squealed as loudly as I could. There was no way I would be getting any sleep tonight.

CHAPTER 6

LISETTE AND I HELD EACH OTHER TIGHTLY ON THE front staircase the next morning.

"I am going to miss you, Lisette."

"I am going to miss you too. Promise to keep in touch?"

"Absolutely."

Jonathon put his arm around me as the royal family and I watched her get into her car and drive out of sight.

"I have a very busy day ahead of me. I probably won't see you until dinner tonight," he said sadly.

"It's okay. I will hang out in the library. It has been a while since I have gotten to read."

He kissed my forehead and left with his father.

I smiled at Queen Leona before I headed to the library.

I ran my finger along the shelves. It felt great to be in there again.

I found a book with a promising summary and sat down in my favorite chair.

A short while later, another individual entered the library and walked along the bottom level across from me. I peeked over my book. *Hugo.* I raised my book a little higher to cover my eyes.

Please just grab a book and get out.

"Hello, Lady Ellena," he said as he sat down on the chair opposite me.

I looked up and gave him a cold hello. I put my eyes back onto the pages.

"How are you enjoying your new title?"

"Very well, thank you," I replied, not looking away from my book, hoping he would get the hint that I did not want to talk.

"It is amazing that you have only been here a couple of weeks and have moved up the social ladder."

Apparently, he was slow on social cues.

I lowered my book. "It's not something I planned."

"Doesn't matter. You obviously have talent."

"Talent has nothing to do with it. I couldn't stand the thought of my friends getting hurt."

"Ah, altruism. A great quality in a leader."

"What are you talking about?"

"You can't tell me that you haven't pictured yourself as queen."

"For your information, I have not."

He got up and started walking around the sitting area with his hands behind his back. I eyed him curiously.

"How about the prince? Have you pictured yourself by his side?"

I looked down, blushing.

"Getting tied down to someone you have only known a couple of weeks." He shook his head. "You realize there are other options, right?"

I snapped my head back up. "Not for me. And we are only dating."

He chuckled. "A royal wouldn't officially date someone unless they were a serious prospect."

Really?

The thought made me smile, but I did not let it show.

"What business is it of yours who I date?"

Creep.

He did not answer my question. "You know, there are some who are not pleased with how King Olov runs Olandia."

I narrowed my eyes. "What are you insinuating?"

He put up his hands in defense. "Nothing. I am simply saying the crown may not be there for Jonathon to receive later."

I did not like what he was hinting at. I stood up. "Are you threatening the royal family?"

"I am not. I am simply stating a fact that many have come to believe." He grinned.

I had to get out of this conversation. I turned to leave. He grabbed my arm. I looked at him, hoping my glare would cover up the underlying terror I felt.

"Changes are coming," he warned.

I yanked my arm free and walked out as fast as I could.

I paced the hall until I saw Hanna.

"Hanna!"

She started waving furiously.

We hugged. "Can you afford a break? I need to talk to you."

"Pfft. I am sure I can afford fifteen minutes," she said, smiling.

I led us to the gardens.

"What are your thoughts about Hugo?" I asked.

"He is a creep! Always keeping to the shadows and just watching people."

"I had the most bizarre run-in with him just now." I recounted the whole conversation to her. "Is it something I should worry about?"

"Hmm. I do not know if what he said counts as a threat. Don't get me wrong. I don't like him or what he said, but he doesn't strike me as the kind smart enough to do something as brazen as taking out the royal family."

We looked at each other and snorted.

"So ... how are things going with *Jonathon*?" she asked while batting her eyelashes.

I shoved her away, giggling. "Things are good. We are officially a couple."

"What!" she squealed. "When did this happen?"

"Just last night, after dinner, when he dropped me off at my door."

She grabbed my arm and jumped up and down, continuing to squeal. "How did he ask?"

"He was so nervous, Han. It was adorable. He asked me to 'join him in official courtship.'"

"Aww." She nudged me. "You are so red, Ell."

"Shut up," I said, weaving my arm through hers.

"Are you all right, Lady Ellena?"

I was still thinking about my conversation with Hugo. Queen Leona's question brought my focus back.

"You haven't touched your soup, dear."

"Sorry, Your Majesty. I am not the biggest fan of seafood," I replied, playing with the oyster floating in the broth.

"What foods do you enjoy?" Jonathon asked.

"Well, I really enjoy Italian food. I could eat an entire pizza by myself."

Jonathon chuckled.

"I also cannot pass up a big, greasy cheeseburger. And sweets? They're my Achille's heel."

Jonathon kept eye contact with me, grinning and looking as if he was soaking in every bit of this new information.

"What about you?" I asked, turning the question back to him.

"I enjoy Italian, same as you. However, I also enjoy seafood quite a bit," he answered.

I shook my head playfully. "Shame. You were such a good boyfriend." We both laughed.

The king cleared his throat.

Jonathon turned to him and apologized. The queen was beaming at the other end.

"What can you tell me about Hugo?" I asked Jonathon as he walked me back to my room.

"What would you like to know?"

"I don't know. Is he a good employee?"

"He seems to be, seeing as how my father has kept him employed for the past ten years."

"Does he seem to enjoy it?"

He snorted. "I don't know. You have seen him. He never looks happy."

I smiled.

"Where is this coming from?"

"I just get weird feelings about him, that's all."

"You are not the only one."

After another sweet good night kiss from him, I got myself ready for bed.

Maybe he is just weird.

I crawled into bed, pushing away any thoughts about Hugo meaning ill will to the royal family.

CHAPTER 7

I STARED AT JONATHON AT BREAKFAST A FEW DAYS later. I loved how the sun outlined his body coming in from the window behind him.

He met my eyes and smiled. I looked down bashfully. I knew we were dating, but we were still basically strangers. Even though I loved our conversations every mealtime, they hardly allowed us to get past the surface. If what Hugo said was true, that royalty only dated those they saw as serious prospects, I felt like we should be getting to know each other on a deeper level.

I was walking the main floor halls, like I did most of the day, every day, since becoming a lady, when I heard a crash come from the kitchen. I ran inside. Glass was all over the floor from a serving bowl. I grabbed the broom and joined the cook in cleaning up the pieces.

"Oh, you don't need to be doing that, ma'am," she said to me, a little shaken.

"It's fine! It's giving me something to do besides wandering around the castle aimlessly." I smiled.

She relaxed slightly.

After we finished cleaning up the mess, I asked, "May I help you with prepping for lunch?"

She looked at me bewildered.

"Seriously, I have got nothing better to do right now."

"Sure, miss. Let me get you an apron. I would hate to see you ruin that pretty dress."

She had me cutting up strawberries as she grilled chicken breast that we would be adding to the salad for lunch.

The strawberries looked so good that I could not help myself. I popped one into my mouth.

"Tsk, tsk, tsk."

I turned to the voice. There was Jonathon, leaning against the side of the door with his arms crossed.

Did he ever not look good?

He walked over. "What if someone had seen?" he asked, popping one into his own mouth.

I nudged him, grinning.

He chuckled.

"What are you doing in here?" he asked.

"I am not used to *not* doing anything. It's nice to have my hands busy."

"I bet that is quite a change for you."

"It really is."

We stood in silence for a moment.

"I feel like we haven't had much time alone. I cleared my schedule for the rest of the day. After lunch, would you mind joining me for a horse ride?"

I could not keep myself from smiling. "I would love to."

Jonathon led me out to the stables. He stopped in front of a stall that had a white horse with light and dark brown blotches all over. They were large and reminded me of the shape of the continents.

"This is Water Canyon. She is very mild mannered and will be good for your first time."

I stuck my hand out, and she nuzzled her nose into it.

"Hey, girl."

He walked over to a different stall with a black horse in it. Her hair was the kind of black that looked blue in certain light.

"This is my horse, Midnight." She nuzzled into his chest as he rubbed the side of her neck. It was clear they had a strong bond.

We led the horses out of the stables and onto the dirt pathway.

Jonathon came up behind me.

"Are you ready?" he asked, placing his hands on my waist. A warm tingle climbed up my back.

I nodded. He hoisted me up onto the saddle.

I was hunched over, gripping the horn for dear life.

He chuckled. "Take a breath and straighten your back … There you go. Now, grab the reins. Make sure to leave a little slack. Perfect."

He got up onto Midnight.

Dang, he looks good on a horse.

I gave Water Canyon a light tap on the side and followed Jonathon on the path. Soon, we had left the castle grounds and were in a lightly wooded area.

He slowed Midnight so that we were riding side by side.

"Are you holding on okay?"

"Barely."

"No one's out here. I won't tell anyone if you swing your leg over."

"Thank you!" I said as I abandoned riding sidesaddle.

"Better?"

"Much."

We came upon a peaceful, little pond.

Jonathon hopped down and tied up Midnight. I followed suit with Water Canyon. I joined him at the edge of the pond. He had his hands in his pockets, looking out over the pond, contemplating something.

"Penny for your thoughts?" I asked, looking up at him.

He continued to stare out across the pond. "This is my favorite place to go. I love the peace and stillness that resides here. It's everything that my life is not. I just feel happy here."

I put my hand on his shoulder. I did not know what to say. I hoped that was comforting enough.

He turned to look at me and took my hands in his, rubbing his fingers across my knuckles. "Whenever I am with you, I feel the same peace and stillness. I just feel happy around you."

I grinned, looking up at him. I put my hand on the side of his face. He leaned his head into it.

"You make me happy too. I feel like I can never get enough of you when you are around, and when you are not, I am yearning for the next time you will be."

The second I finished speaking, his lips were on mine. He pulled me close and wrapped his arms tightly across my back. I moved my hand that was on his face, up into his hair, running my fingers through it. My other arm was wrapped across his lower back. He parted his lips, slightly pulling in mine.

Oh my gosh.

If he had not been holding onto me, I would have collapsed onto the ground. We continued sliding our lips over the other's and moving our hands up and down each other's back.

We pulled away breathless and stared at each other, slowly catching it again.

He cupped my face with his hand. "I know we have only known each other a few weeks, but I care about you, Ellena."

Gosh I loved hearing him say my name.

I pulled him down into another kiss. "I care about you too."

We sat down at the water's edge, took off our shoes, and let our feet rest in the shallow water. Part of the time, we talked and laughed. Other times, we sat in comfortable silence.

When it was time for us to head back, he tied Water Canyon to the back of Midnight and pulled me up to sit in front of him. I rested my head against his chest.

He smelled divine. It was a clean yet powerful scent, like wet cypress. I took a deep breath, taking in his smell. He rested his head on mine. We stayed like that all the way back to the castle.

It was getting dark when we arrived back. We returned the horses to the stable and headed toward the dining room, hand in hand. The king and queen were already there. Jonathon pulled out my chair and then walked over and sat in his spot.

"How was your afternoon?" Queen Leona asked, looking between the two of us.

"Wonderful," I replied, glancing at Jonathon, who was doing the same.

"Yes, wonderful," he agreed, smiling.

We ate in silence for a few minutes.

"Lady Ellena, I would love it if you would join me for tea tomorrow," she said to me.

I looked back to her. "I would love to, Your Majesty."

She smiled, going back to her appetizer.

"Uh oh," King Olov declared.

"What?" Queen Leona looked at her husband.

"It is never good for us men when you women get together for tea. It is nothing but giggling and gossiping and ..." He shuddered.

"Oh, hush, you." She playfully slapped her husband.

They were darling together. I hoped to still be that playful that far along in marriage.

With Jonathon? Perhaps.

I could not settle my mind. I stared at the ceiling, recalling our date that afternoon. It. Was. Perfect. I had not realized I cared for him that deeply until he confessed the same to me. I was feeling myself fall, and it was fast and hard.

CHAPTER 8

"IT SEEMS OUR DEAR PRINCE JONATHON HAS FOUND himself someone special, but who is she?" King Olov read from the newspaper at breakfast.

Jonathon and I glanced up at each other and smiled.

"This humble columnist hopes that she makes herself known to the rest of the country at the annual peach festival!" the king continued.

I paused eating.

"What do you say, Prince Jonathon? May we meet your special lady?" he finished.

I looked back up at Jonathon. He caught my eye.

"I think it's a great idea!" King Olov said.

I turned my attention to him.

Uh …

"I agree, dear," Queen Leona echoed.

My eyes moved to her.

Oh, come on …

"I do too," Jonathon added.

I stared at him with wide eyes.

What the …

"I am excited to show off the girl who holds my attention and my heart."

Aww … Dang it, he is smooth.

Honestly, why did I even think this was not going to happen? I could not stay in the shadows forever. He was the prince, and anyone close to him would be known to the people.

"Then it is settled," King Olov said as he got up from the table.

There was a brief pause.

"So, um, what am I supposed to do during the festival?" I asked nervously.

"Don't worry, dear. We will go into it during tea today." She beamed at me.

That helped me relax a little. "Wonderful."

"You will do great, Ellena," Jonathon added with a confident smile.

I walked out into the garden later that morning and saw the queen already sitting at the table, holding an umbrella, shading herself from the sun. There was a slight breeze, making her waves dance on her shoulders. Her beautiful appearance coupled with her grace and poise made her the epitome of classy.

"Your Majesty," I said, giving her a curtsy.

"Lady Ellena." She motioned to chair I should take.

She waved over the servant with the tray that contained the tea and cookies.

"Since it is an outside event, it has been customary for the ladies to wear summer dresses," she started.

I nodded. "Okay."

"I recommend wearing short heels or flats. Otherwise, your feet will be killing you by the end of the day."

Not a problem.

"Do you have a sunhat?" she asked.

"I do."

"Good. The public looks down on us wearing sunglasses. They feel it makes us seem distant."

"I can understand that."

"When standing, keep your legs together. When sitting, always cross your legs or ankles."

"Okay."

"Never fold your arms. Simply lay your hands on top of each other."

Crap. That is going to be a problem.

"They are curious about you, so they are going to bombard you with questions. Try to answer several of them, but once you get tired of them, just say, 'That is all for now.'"

I nodded.

Man, I hope I remember all of this.

As if hearing my thoughts, she said, "Don't worry, dear. You will do great." She gave me a smile.

"Thank you, Your Majesty."

She took a bite of her cookie.

"Now, to get to the main reason why I wanted to have tea with you today. How are things going with Jonathon?"

I choked on the sip of tea I had just taken. "Very good, Your Majesty." I could tell I was blushing.

Unsatisfied with my answer, she kindly prodded for more. "In what ways?"

I looked down at the table. "Well … I am used to feeling invisible. He makes me feel seen."

She was beaming at me.

"He seems to really care about the people. I admire that."

She nodded. "He does. Very much."

I could feel my face reddening with that I was going to say next. "He is incredibly handsome, so I find it hard to keep my eyes off of him."

She giggled. "He takes after his father."

"I see bits of you in him too, like the slight wave in his hair and his kind eyes." I looked off into the distance, imagining him.

I looked back at her.

She was looking at me, deep in thought. "You care about him, don't you?"

"I do, Your Majesty."

"Good, because he feels the same for you."

Even though I already knew that because of our date yesterday, I still blushed at hearing it again.

The rest of our visit was less serious. We chatted about many subjects.

I came to learn that we had a lot of things in common, like our love for the garden and weakness for sweets. It was nice to get to know her on a more personal level. I bet she was wonderful to have as a mother. If things went that way with Jonathon and me, she would become a mother figure to me.

I smiled at the thought.

"What is it, dear?"

"Nothing, Your Majesty. Just thank you for this wonderful afternoon."

"I am scared out of my mind!" I told Hanna at lunch. "Yes, I feel *a little* better after the pep talk but *only* a little."

"I agree with Her Majesty and the prince; you will do great."

"You are my best friend, Hanna. Don't lie to me. Do you see me messing it up?"

She paused. "As long as you don't try to turn and run from anyone, you should be fine." She started laughing. I smacked her arm.

"What duty did Miriam give you for the festival?"

"I will be handing out champagne," she answered, smiling.

"I should get to see you a lot then."

"You should."

We grinned.

"I wish I could see you more often than I get to," I said, sadly.

"Me too."

We sat in silence for a moment.

"Hey! I have an idea! Do you have a maid yet?"

I knew exactly what she was hinting at. "Hanna, you're a genius! I will ask Their Majesties at dinner tonight."

I could not sit down and read a book like I usually did because I was ecstatic at the possibility of Hanna being my maid, so I decided to walk around the third-floor halls.

We would be around each other constantly. To avoid the awkwardness of her serving me, I would limit my requests of her. I would be content just having her around me, doing each other's hair, and talking nonstop.

Even though I had been there almost a month, I still did not know whose rooms were whose. The walls were nice and thick, so I couldn't hear voices from the adjoining rooms. Queen Leona was usually either outside in the garden or on the main floor, and the king and Jonathon were usually on the second floor in meetings all day long. I had not gotten the courage to walk the second floor yet, since I felt that they would appreciate the privacy.

The door ahead was cracked open.

Do I dare peek in?

Curiosity got the best of me. I put my face in the crack and looked around the room. At first, it seemed like no one was in there. Then a figure walked in front of the glass balcony doors and stopped, facing them. I knew that outline.

I tapped on the door lightly. Jonathon turned around, and his face lit up when he saw it was me.

"Ellena! Please come in."

I stepped in. "Would you like me to leave the door open or shut it?"

"You can shut it."

He put down a stack of papers he was holding and gave me his attention.

"What can I do for you?" he asked, leaning back against the window.

"I don't know. I was just wandering the halls when I saw your door cracked open and decided to take a peek. I guess I just could not walk away after seeing it was you in here," I replied, half laughing.

He stood up, putting his arms straight out to his sides. "Would you like the grand tour?"

"I would," I said, smiling.

I took his outstretched arm as he led me around his room.

"This is my closet, where I put all of my clothes."

"No way! I have one of those too!"

"You don't say!"

We laughed.

"These are the doors to my balcony." He threw them open with flair.

My jaw dropped. "Wow …"

"Do you like the view?"

I looked out over the buildings of the capital. "I do. I have never seen the city from a view like this."

"Would you like me to switch your rooms to a city view?"

"No! Thank you, but I quite enjoy my garden view."

"Shall we?" he asked, starting up the tour again. That was the silliest I had ever seen Jonathon be. I had not known he had that side to him. I liked it.

He led me to the middle of the room, where he stopped at the end of his bed. It had to be twice as big as mine and looked twice as comfortable.

"And this is my bed." He paused, shifting uncomfortably. "Where I sleep and stuff."

I looked at him curiously. "What is the other *stuff* you do on your bed?" I asked, trying to make him squirm some more. It worked.

"Oh, nothing fun yet," he said quickly, trying to get out of the awkward conversation.

"Yet, huh?"

He was making this too easy.

"Oh my gosh! That's not what I meant!" He was beet red.

I started laughing.

"You're enjoying this, aren't you?"

"Just a little."

I abandoned torturing him and walked around to one of his end tables. There was a stack of books: *History of Olandia, The Art of Persuasive Speaking,* and *The Art of War.*

"It's pretty serious, isn't it?" I asked, turning back to him.

He had his hands in his pockets, his face sullen. He nodded.

There was a knock on the door.

"Prince Jonathon? Your father is requesting your presence," the voice from the other side of the door stated.

"Thank you. Tell him I will be right there."

He walked over to me.

"I am afraid I must go."

I nodded.

He took my hands into his and kissed them.

"Enjoy your afternoon, Lady Ellena."

"You too, Your Highness."

The men were unusually quiet at dinner. I desperately wanted to talk with Jonathon, but I did not want to interrupt his thoughts. I had an idea. I hoped he picked up on it.

I stood from my chair. "Thank you for dinner, Your Majesties. I am going to walk the gardens before heading to bed. Good night."

I looked at Jonathon and gave him a slight smile. I was met with a bigger one.

He got it.

He joined me on the bench by the fountain a few minutes later.

"I know you probably can't tell me anything, but if I can help in any way with all that is going on, please let me know."

He pulled my hand over to him and started tracing designs on the back of it.

"The night of the ball, there were two shooters. Our guards fired back, but they escaped unharmed."

I sat in silence, letting him continue.

"We have sent out search parties to look for this group, but our efforts have been in vain. There has been total silence for the past couple of weeks, no regular threatening letters like they usually do. We are worried that another attack is coming. We are nervous about the peach festival tomorrow."

He looked up at me, searching my expression.

Great. Now I was terrified.

"I am assuming you have already increased the numbers of guards."

He nodded.

"There is not much else you *can* do. It's a public event. You also can't cancel it since it is tradition."

"Our thoughts exactly."

We sat in silence for a while.

"I completely forgot to ask at dinner, but may I request a personal maid?"

"Of course. I will assign someone to you immediately."

"Thank you, but I already have someone in mind—if that's okay?"

Hanna came bursting in my room, squealing, later that night. We wrapped each other up in a tight hug. Jonathon stood in the doorway, smiling.

I walked over to him and wrapped my arms around him.

"Thank you." I looked up, and he leaned down to give me a kiss.

"You're welcome."

We stared at each other for a few moments.

"A-hem," Hanna muttered.

"I am going to help her settle in. Good night, Jonathon."

"Good night, Ellena."

I shut the door and joined Hanna on my bed, where we stayed up and talked half of the night.

CHAPTER 9

"IF YOU DON'T FEEL COMFORTABLE, DON'T FEEL LIKE you are obligated to be there," I told Hanna as she curled my hair.

"Are you kidding? I have always gone to the peach festival. I am not going to miss it because some would-be assassins may or may not be there."

"I am going to greatly appreciate your presence," I said, grabbing her hand. "I am more terrified of the press than I am of the assassins. Is that weird?"

"Nope! I don't envy you today at all."

I stood up and walked to the full-length mirror. The dress was white with rose blossoms and their accompanying stems stamped all over it. The sleeves were sheer and lightweight. The dress came in at my waist and went out loose and flowy down to a little past my knees. I put on the matching white sunhat and flats. I turned to Hanna.

"How do I look for my first press butchering?"

"Like a lamb to the slaughter. You look gorgeous."

"Thank you. I need to stop by Jonathon's room. He wanted to see my dress so he could pick out a matching dress shirt. See you at the festival."

His door was cracked again, and I gave it a tap. He opened it almost immediately.

My jaw dropped as I scanned down his muscular, *shirtless* chest.

Have mercy.

"You look lovely," he said, snapping my focus back.

"Thank you." I swished my skirt. "What shirt do you have in mind?"

Or lack thereof.

He turned and headed toward his closet. His back was just as muscular as his front.

Is it hot in here?

He came out in a green shirt that matched the rose stems.

"What do you think?" he asked, holding out his arms with the shirt still unbuttoned.

"You look good," I answered, looking across his torso.

I looked down and cleared my throat.

"Do you mind helping me with this?" he asked.

I walked over and started at the bottom of the shirt, fumbling with every other button. I could feel him shaking from stifling his laughter. I looked up at him.

"You're enjoying this, aren't you?"

"Just a little."

I shook my head, smiling, and finished buttoning his shirt. He tucked it in and offered his arm.

"Shall we?"

I nodded, taking his arm.

The main doors were wide open, showing the crowd of people waiting for us to come out.

I took a deep breath.

He put his hand on my arm. "Are you ready?"

"As ready as I will ever be."

We walked through the doors and into the sunlight. The crowd exploded into flashes of light and overlapping questions and exclamations.

I put on a polite smile, and Jonathon waved. We walked down the steps and stopped at the bottom, letting the crowd know we were ready for questions.

"What is your name?" a woman directed toward me.

"Lady Ellena Petersson."

"How long have you been dating?" another asked.

We looked at each other and smiled.

"One week," I answered.

"How long have you guys known each other?" yet another asked.

Jonathon took this one. "Almost a month."

"How are you settling into the castle?" yet *another* asked.

"Smoothly."

"Are you looking forward to the festival today?" the first woman asked.

"Yes, we are," I answered.

"And with that, we would like to join everyone else. Thank you." Jonathon led us away from the reporters.

"My head is spinning," I whispered as we headed out into the rest of the crowd.

He chuckled. "Yeah, it can be pretty bad sometimes. You will get used to it."

I will, huh?

We found the king and queen standing under a tree and joined them.

"How did your first interrogation go?" Queen Leona asked.

"I think I did well." I looked to Jonathon for confirmation.

"Yes, you did," he agreed, smiling down at me.

"Wonderful. You guys go enjoy the festival. We will see you later for the toast." She nodded toward the rest of the festival.

"What would you like to do first?" Jonathon asked.

I took a deep breath in through my nose. "Whatever that vendor is making smells divine." I nodded at a nearby food truck.

"Sounds good."

We got up to the window.

"What are you serving today, sir?" Jonathon asked the middle-aged man.

"What we have here, Your Highness, is a braised brisket with a bourbon-peach glaze."

"Excellent. We will take two please."

Jonathon led us to a table nearby while we waited for our order. We did not have to wait long; the vendor practically followed us over.

He placed our food down in front of us. "Enjoy!"

"Thank you so much," Jonathon said.

"Yes, thank you," I added.

The vendor bowed and went back to his truck.

I cut off a slice of the brisket and put it in my mouth. It started to disintegrate immediately but not before the explosion of the sweet and bitter sauce danced across my tongue.

"Mmmm." I groaned to myself.

"It's delicious, isn't it?"

"So delicious."

We were not able to talk much during our meal because of Jonathon's passing admirers. He was adored by his people. Some were kind enough to address me as well.

Once we finished, I stated, "Your turn."

He grabbed my hand and started walking toward the rides. "Let's go on my favorite ride: the Ferris wheel."

I hid a gulp. I hated heights.

We climbed into the waiting car. Jonathon put his arm around me, and I snuggled into his body.

He grinned. "Getting cozy, are we?"

"Yes and no. I am terrified of heights."

The ride jerked into motion. I buried my face into his chest and wrapped my outside arm around his stomach. He wrapped both of his arms around me, pulling me close.

We went around a few times, and then it came to a stop. I was not stupid. I knew what that meant. We were at the very top. I kept my face buried in his chest.

"Look," he whispered. "I have got you."

I lifted my head and opened my eyes. The view was incredible, albeit terrifying.

I looked around at the bustling festival all around. There had to be hundreds of people walking around. When my eyes came upon the castle and I saw we were the same height as Jonathon's bedroom, I squealed and hid my head again.

He laughed.

The ride jolted again, and we headed back down.

"Okay," I said, rubbing the sweat off my hands onto my dress. "Now for *my* favorite ride: the eggbeaters."

We climbed into a seat, and I directed him to sit by me as far inside of the seat as we could be. The safety bar was lowered, and the ride started.

"This isn't so bad," Jonathon stated.

"Just wait."

The ride picked up its pace, and we started slowly moving down the seat. We both gripped the bar, trying to slow our slide over.

"This is crazy!" He laughed.

"I love it!" he shouted over the noise of the other riders.

"Let go!"

"What?"

"Just do it!"

We both let go and slid violently into the other side. We both burst out laughing and stayed that way until the ride ended.

We climbed out clumsily and found a bench to sit on until we caught our breath.

"I'm thirsty. Would you like a drink?" he asked.

"I would love one." We made our way to a fresh-squeezed peach lemonade stand.

"How do you feel about a hayride through the orchard?" He held out his arm.

"It sounds great."

We were the last ones on the cart and filled it to max capacity. Everyone was looking at us, whispering, and trying but miserably failing at secretively taking pictures on their phones. Jonathon seemed perfectly comfortable with all the attention. I, however, wanted to make like an ostrich and bury my head in the dirt.

The cart jolted forward. I fell over onto Jonathon, giggling.

"Sorry."

He put his arm around me, grinning.

"If you wanted to snuggle, you could have just asked." He winked.

"Har, har."

We leaned back against the railing and settled in for the ride. We followed a path that took us right in the middle of a fully bloomed peach orchard. The air was cooler and smelled deliciously of ripened peaches. The tall green trees were spotted with little red to orange to yellow ombre circles.

"Would you like one?"

"What?" Jonathon's question caught me off guard.

"Would you like one?" he repeated.

Not sure what he was meaning, I answered cautiously. "Sure ..."

Before I knew what was happening, he hopped off the cart, grabbed a peach off the ground, and hopped back on.

"For you, my lady."

I took it. "Thank you, Your Highness, but was that allowed?"

"I don't see a problem with it, but even if there was, you are worth breaking rules for." He gave a smile that made my heart want to beat out of my chest.

I smiled and took a bite out of the best peach I had ever tasted. Whether it was because the peach itself was perfect or because of who gave it to me, I didn't know, and I didn't care.

"That is delicious. Would you like a bite?" I asked, holding out the peach to him.

He leaned over and took a bite.

He groaned. "Delicious."

We stared at each other for a moment. We began glancing at each other's lips, heading toward a kiss, when a little voice interrupted.

"Prince Jonathon? Can I get a picture with you?" a little girl with big blue eyes asked.

"Absolutely!"

They wrapped their arms around each other, and her mother took a picture.

"Can I ask you another question?" she bashfully asked.

"Of course."

"When the hayride is over, do you mind coming to the field and playing soccer with my friends and I?"

Jonathon looked at me, looking for an answer.

"This I have to see," I said.

"Sounds like a plan. See you there," he answered, smiling.

"Yay!" She bounced back to her mother.

"Are you good at soccer?"

"Not. At. All," he whispered.

I laughed. "Now I am *really* excited to see this."

We made our way over to the field where several little kids waited for Jonathon.

The same little girl stepped forward, took his hand, and pulled him toward the group of kids in the middle of the field. Jonathon rolled up his sleeves as they divided into two teams and got ready for the ball to drop. Once it was put into play, they all scrambled after it. The little blue-eyed girl took off down the field with it.

Dang, she is good!

She scored it into the net on her first try. Her team erupted with cheers.

As Jonathon's team started heading down the other way, I noticed a small group of people had gathered around the field to watch.

A little boy on Jonathon's team shouted for the ball. Johnathon passed the ball to him, and he scored. Their team cheered.

As the game continued, more and more people gathered. Reporters had pulled out their cameras and were taking pictures.

Near the end, the score was 3–4, with Jonathon's team behind. It was their turn for a last try to get a goal.

Jonathon had the ball and a clear shot into the net. He kicked it wide. His team moaned, and the other cheered. He gave them all high fives as the crowd clapped. He made his way to me.

"How was I?" he asked, trying to catch his breath.

"I thought you did great, especially with that last shot." I smiled knowingly.

He winked.

He was sweaty, and his hair stuck to his head.

Mmm hmm.

He looked at his watch. "It is almost time for the toast. We should be heading back."

I took his outstretched arm and helped him look for his parents.

We found them near the bottom of the castle steps, holding

wine glasses. As we approached, a reporter asked for a picture of them, and King Olov put his glass down on a step. They turned and smiled for the picture.

I picked up his glass and was waiting to hand it back to him when he grabbed a new one from a passing tray. I turned to give it to Jonathon but saw he had one now as well.

I guess I will drink it.

King Olov raised his arms, beckoning the crowd to quiet down.

"This has been another wonderful peach festival, and I would like to recognize all of those who made it the spectacle that it was." He clapped, and we all followed suit.

"I am pleased that we did not let a small group of terrorists ruin our annual celebration." The crowd clapped again. "I would like to toast to Olandia, her people, and one of her finest exports, her peaches." We all raised our glasses and took a sip.

Yuck! That is bitter.

I tried to shake away the nasty flavor sitting in my mouth.

"Have a wonderful summer, Olandia!" The crowd erupted into cheers.

My throat started to feel tight. I cleared my throat, hoping it would help. It did not. It started to burn. I brought my hand up to my neck.

"Ellena? Are you okay?" Jonathon asked, worried.

I shook my head. "My throat feels funny."

He took my glass from me and smelled it.

His eyes widened. "Father!"

He handed the glass to the king, who shared a worried look with him.

It was getting hard to breathe. They both looked at me. I turned and started walking up the steps to the castle. I needed water.

I started to feel lightheaded, and my vision blurred. I almost fell against the doorway. Instead, Jonathon had his arm around me, holding me up.

"Ellena, I need you to hang on," he pleaded, walking us farther into the castle.

I looked up at him and only caught a glimpse of the panic on his face before everything went black.

CHAPTER 10

"CHANGES ARE COMING." HUGO'S WARNING ECHOED in the darkness. I felt a chill run through me. I needed to warn the royal family. Was I alive? I looked for someone, anyone.

No one.

Was I dead? I looked for a light.

Nothing.

The darkness started closing in on me. I tried to run. I could not tell if it was working since I was surrounded by the same degree of darkness. I started weeping, quietly at first, then louder and louder.

"Help!" I screamed.

I waited for an answer.

"Help!"

Silence.

I collapsed in defeat.

I felt a tingle in my left hand. I looked at it. Even though no one was there, it distinctly felt like someone was holding it. I tried to move my hand, but it was stuck in a cupping position as if someone else's hand was in it.

Jonathon.

"Wake up, Ellena! Please wake up!" I yelled to myself.

"Wake up, Ellena. Please wake up." This time, it was Jonathon's voice.

I felt myself being pulled out of the darkness.

I blinked my eyes open, squinting at the light that came pouring into them.

I groaned.

I looked to my left and saw Jonathon there, holding my hand. His eyes immediately switched from worry to relief.

"Oh, Ellena!" He grabbed my face with his other hand and kissed me urgently.

He leaned his forehead on mine. "I thought I was going to lose you."

I put my other hand on his face. "I am very stubborn," I whispered, grinning.

He pulled away, and I saw that he had stubble covering his jaw and above his lips.

How long was I out?

As if reading my thoughts, he said, "You were out for three days."

I went to sit up, but the dizziness knocked me back down.

"Maybe not yet." I chuckled.

"Yes. You take it easy." He put his hand on my face. I leaned into it, and he stroked my cheek.

"That drink was meant for my father," he whispered.

I pulled up my most recent memories.

It was.

"I am so sorry, Ellena."

"Hey," I whispered. "It wasn't your fault."

He closed his eyes, and a tear escaped. He wiped it away with his shoulder.

We sat in silence for several moments.

I wanted to take away his pain, his unnecessary guilt. My heart ached seeing him like that. I never wanted to see him like that again.

He took a deep, shaky breath. "I know we have not known

each other long … but … since you entered my life, I have not wanted you to leave it. I want to be with you all the time, and when I can't be, you are on my mind constantly. If there was ever any thought in my mind that I would be okay if you walked out of my life, it's gone. I would not be okay. I would be anything but … I need you, Ellena." He scooted off the chair he was sitting on and onto the floor, kneeling.

Oh. My. Gosh.

My heart was banging against my ribs.

He put one hand into his pocket and pulled out a small box.

Holy crap.

He opened it, revealing a single, princess-cut stone shining up at me. Simple. Perfect.

"Ellena Petersson, will you do me the great honor of becoming Ellena Larsson? The future queen of Olandia … the queen of my heart."

My eyes stung with tears as I barely squeaked out a breathy "Yes!" and he placed the ring on my finger. I put my hands on each side of his face and brought his lips to mine. He sat down on the bed and wrapped his arms around me. It was the sweetest kiss we had ever shared.

"So much for taking it easy. I could run around the castle right now." I chuckled.

He let out a laugh. "There is someone who is going to be livid with me for not bringing them in right when you woke up. I will go get her."

Hanna came running into the room a few minutes later. She came over and wrapped me in a hug, threatening to suffocate me.

"I was terrified that you were not going to make it!" she said, struggling to hold back tears.

"You should know me better than that. Did you really think a little poison was going to take me away and let you have all the fun?"

We chuckled.

She pulled back, and we sat in silence for a moment.

"So, did you enjoy the festival?" I asked, breaking the silence.

She nodded. "Until that last part." She gave a weak smile. "Did you?"

"Very much so … until that last part." We snorted.

I leaned my head back against the headboard.

"If someone would've told me that I was going to be a victim of poisoning a month ago, I would've thought they were crazy."

"Right? So much has changed in just a month." She looked down. I watched her gaze fall onto my left hand. Her eyes went wide. She grabbed my hand and held it up.

"Are you freaking serious?" she squealed.

I could only smile and nod my head.

She screamed, wrapping me in a hug again.

Jonathon burst into the room. "Is everything okay?"

Hanna and I looked at him. She hopped off the bed and gave him a hug.

"Oh …" He did not know what to do. I showed him my hand.

"Ahh …" He hugged her back.

She pulled away. "I am so sorry, Your Highness!" She gave him a curtsy. "I am just excited; that is all."

He grinned at me. "It's okay. So am I."

Jonathon thought it would be a good idea for me to take my dinner in bed. I was more than okay with the idea.

He placed the tray over my lap and removed the cover. I stared down at the medium-rare steak smothered in grilled onions and mushrooms, with a side of loaded mashed potatoes, Waldorf salad, and a baguette. I inhaled the steam coming off the food. My stomach growled. I. Was. Starving.

Jonathon sat next to me on the bed with his own dinner. I was grateful that it was just the two of us because I knew that my eating was going to be anything but ladylike.

I cut off a big chunk of steak, dunked it into the mashed potatoes, and put it into my mouth.

"Mmmm." I groaned with my eyes closed.

Jonathon chuckled, kissed me on the temple, then started eating his dinner.

We ate in silence for a few minutes.

"I need to tell you something," I said with a mouthful of food.

"Okay …" Jonathon warily answered.

"I had a strange conversation with Hugo about a week ago. He said that there are people displeased with your father and that changes are coming."

Jonathon put his silverware down and let out a deep sigh. "That is nerve-wracking to hear, but it does not prove that he has been behind anything. I will make my father aware of this immediately after dinner, and we will keep a close eye on Hugo."

He wrapped his arm around me, and I leaned into him.

I hope Hugo does not catch on.

I felt well enough to get out of bed and walk around a couple days later. Since King Olov, Queen Leona, and Jonathon could not change their routines too much or Hugo would pick up on it, we all decided that I should be the main one to keep an eye on Hugo. I, of course, enlisted Hanna's help.

We were in the library.

"We get to be spies?" she exclaimed quietly.

"Yes, but this is serious, Hanna. Whoever is targeting the king, whether that be Hugo or not, is smart and dangerous. We need to be careful," I cautioned.

"Of course." Some of her excitement disappeared.

"Do you know which room is his?" I asked.

She nodded.

"We need to get in there and look around. Do you know the times he is not there?"

"I'm not positive. I know he is usually kept quite busy during the day."

"Hmm. Do you mind finding out where he is from Miriam?"

She gave me a mock salute. "Double-o Hanna is on the case."

Before I could reprimand her again, she was out of the library.

I sat down in my chair, trying to keep myself calm.

A few minutes passed. I stood up and started pacing back and forth.

How is she going to figure this out without giving us away?

She walked in a couple minutes later, looking proud of herself.

"I'm assuming you know where he is?" I asked her, cocking an eyebrow.

She nodded, beaming. "He will be in a meeting on the second floor for the next half hour."

"Then let's get going."

We got to the top of the stairs that led down to the servants' quarters.

"I think you should go down, Hanna. It will look less suspicious since you still live down there."

She nodded in agreement.

"I will stay here and keep watch. We need a signal if I see him coming. What should it be?"

"How about a cough? It would echo through the halls. I would have no trouble hearing it."

"Sounds good. Be careful, Han." I gave her a hug.

She smiled and headed down the stairs.

I did not know what to do with myself. I tried leaning against the wall.

No … I look like I am up to something.

I tried walking in an inconspicuous line near the stairs.

No … I look like I am waiting for something. Which is exactly what I am doing!

I found a picture along the wall nearby. I stood in front of it, pretending to look at it.

I saw Hugo heading down the stairs at the end of the hall.

What? He is done early!

I casually walked back over to the stairs and let out a loud cough.

About fifteen seconds passed, and no Hanna. Hugo was getting closer. I leaned down the stairs and coughed again.

Ten seconds passed. No Hanna. Luckily, Hugo turned into the kitchen.

I took advantage of this and ran down the stairs. I did not know which room was his. I coughed loudly again, scanning all of the doors.

Finally, a door opened, and out came Hanna. I motioned for her to hurry back.

Right as we exited the top of the stairs, there was Hugo.

We jumped.

"Ladies …" he said, eyeing us suspiciously.

"Sir," we answered together, giving a curtsy, then walking away. I could feel his eyes on us.

That was close.

We locked the door once we made it back to my room.

"So, what did you find?" I asked.

"At first, I was not finding anything. That is why I did not come out the first two times. I knew I was pressing my luck, but I knew there had to be something. I finally found something taped on the back of his vanity mirror. It was a document called 'The New Order.' I was only able to glance over it. It mentioned things like 'new leadership,' 'secrecy,' and 'allegiance.' I did not think it was a good idea to take it, so I put it back when I heard the third cough. I am sorry." She looked down, ashamed.

"Hey. You have no reason to be sorry! You did great! We now have a lead!"

I was getting situated in my seat at the table when I felt eyes on me. I looked around. The king and queen were both looking at me. I stared back, glancing between the two of them.

What?

I was about to say that out loud when Queen Leona excitedly asked, "May we see it?"

Duh!

"Of course!" I held out my hand across the table. Queen Leona held my hand, smiling widely, while King Olov got up and shook hands with Jonathon and then pulled him into a hug.

"Congratulations, my boy."

"Thank you, Father." Jonathon looked at me. He was beaming. I could feel I was too.

They sat down, and we began dinner.

A little while later, I cleared my throat. "Your Majesties, I have some news of a private nature."

King Olov nodded and waved away the guards and servants, who scattered around the room.

"My friend Hanna went into Hugo's room while he was away today. She found a document that was titled 'The New Order' and contained words such as 'new leadership,' 'secrecy,' and 'allegiance.' She was not able to get details because Hugo was headed our way."

King Olov leaned back into his chair, interlocking his fingers across his stomach. "I want us to keep a closer eye on Hugo. Position a guard down in the servants' hallway. Alert all of the guards to report any suspicious activity that he does."

Jonathon nodded in agreement and left to do his father's commands.

"Thank you for finding out this information, Lady Ellena. It is most appreciated," King Olov said, giving me a slight bow.

I returned it. "Absolutely, Your Majesty."

CHAPTER 11

QUEEN LEONA ASKED FOR ME TO JOIN HER FOR A walk around the gardens after breakfast.

"I would like to throw a ball in honor of your and Jonathon's engagement," she said, smiling.

"I would love that, Your Majesty."

"Wonderful. I will call in my decorators. Would you mind joining me tomorrow to pick out everything for it?"

"Absolutely, Your Majesty!"

There was a pause.

"I have wanted to thank you for being so welcoming to me. I had always heard of your kindness, but I didn't understand the magnitude of it."

She broke into a wide smile. "Thank you, dear." She reached over and squeezed my hand for a moment before we finished our walk in silence.

I went into the kitchen to grab a drink. I noticed Hugo walk briskly past the kitchen doors.

Is he up to anything?

I peeked around the kitchen wall and saw him heading up the stairs. I decided to follow him but kept a good distance between us. He exited onto the second floor. I hid behind the wall and watched him enter a door at the far end of the hall. I was about to head down there when someone called my name.

"Ellena?" It was Jonathon.

I turned and smiled at him as he approached. He put his arm around my waist and pulled me in for a side kiss.

"How are your meetings going?" I asked.

"About as good as they always are. *Very boring.*" He mouthed the last part.

I giggled.

"Are you doing anything right now?" he asked.

I looked down at the end of the hall, then back at him. "No."

He held out his arm. "Come with me. I want to show you something."

He led us to the third floor and into a bedroom. It was the largest one I had seen yet.

"Once we get married, this would become my room, and this one . . ." He walked me over to a door and opened it to reveal a more femininely decorated room. "Would be yours."

Wow.

I went inside and looked around. The closet was twice the size of the one I had, the vanity too. All the furniture was sturdy and heavy. There was not only a balcony but two large windows as well, one to either side. The room was filled with light, not only because the sun was pouring in but also because it was reflected off every surface.

I slid my hand along the edge of the bed draped in silk.

"Do we have to have separate bedrooms?" I could feel heat rise into my cheeks. I looked over to him.

He was blushing as well, looking down and tracing his foot along the ground. "We do not have to, no."

"I understand the propriety and tradition, but …" I walked over to him and grabbed his hands. "I know I am going to want to spend a lot of time with you." I looked down, feeling my heart bang inside my chest.

He tipped my head up to look into his eyes. "I will too." There was a look in his eyes I had not seen before. It made me want to melt.

He moved his hand to the back of my neck and pulled me in for a kiss. It was harder, faster, more fervent. A groan involuntarily escaped me.

I could feel him smile against my lips. I wrapped my arms around his neck, deepening the kiss. He wrapped his arms around my waist and picked me up off the floor.

My body was trembling with excitement. It was hard to breathe. I loved it.

We broke apart, each of us gasping for breath. We stared into each other's eyes.

"We need to get out of here before I do something that will require that bed to be remade."

I looked at him. "What if I don't want to leave?" I asked seriously.

I saw his resolve crumble for a second, and then he shook his head. "I will not dishonor you like that." He gave me a small smile.

I let out a sigh and returned the smile.

Such the gentleman. Dang it.

He put me down, and we walked out of our soon-to-be bedrooms, hand in hand.

The first item on the party agenda was food. Queen Leona and I sat in the dining room while dish after dish was brought for us to sample. The queen preferred the shrimp tartlets, while I fancied the mini burgers. We agreed that the grilled chicken bruschetta was going to be a crowd pleaser.

Next up was wine tasting. We had a difficult time picking. They all tasted delicious! In the end, we picked the chardonnay.

We had to be in the main hall for the next part, and I felt like it was going to take the rest of the day: decorations.

We were presented with a dozen different colors to choose from for the tablecloth and runners. The queen chose a deep purple tablecloth, while I chose a gold runner.

Some of the things we had to choose made sense to me, like what color banners should hang from the windows or what songs should be played by the chamber orchestra.

Others, it took all that I had not to roll my eyes at. I did not care what pattern the napkins were in at the ends of the tables or if the candles should be in a pillar or tumbler jar.

I was in the middle of these types of questions when I saw Hugo bustling up the stairs again. I excused myself and climbed the stairs after him. The second-floor hall was empty. Luckily, I remembered which door he went in yesterday.

I could hear voices talking inside. I put my ear to the door. I was only there a second before I felt hands yank me from the door and push me against the wall next to the room, holding tight onto my arms.

"What the?"

Hugo.

I froze.

"Why are you following me?" he asked, annoyed.

Would lying work at this point?

"Answer me!" he growled, shaking me.

"We know you are the one behind all of the assassination attempts on the king," I said, trying to hide my nervousness.

He chuckled. "That doesn't matter. Things have already been set into motion. We just have to speed things up a little."

He came closer, our faces almost touching. "I have wanted this for a long time." He put his mouth by my ear and whispered, "And I *always* get what I want."

I kneed him in the gut. When his grip on me loosened, I took off running. I turned and saw him fumbling after me. I was headed toward the stairs to go down. I did not think he would follow me into a crowded room.

As I was about to descend, I saw my way was blocked by servants unrolling a carpet at the bottom. I paused and turned around to check on Hugo. He was now walking briskly after me. I decided to run up the stairs to the third floor. If I could make it to my room, I could lock the door.

I was almost to my room when he grabbed my arm. I quickly turned around and tried to punch him in the face. He caught my arm. I immediately kicked my leg up and straight into his groin. He groaned and fell down. I looked down at him, but instead of black hair on a stick-thin body, I saw brown hair on a muscular body.

Jonathon!

My hands flew up to my face and cupped my mouth. I collapsed next to him.

"Jonathon! I am so sorry!"

He looked up at me with pained eyes. "What … was … that … for?"

"I thought you were Hugo! He found out, Jonathon! He had me against the wall. I broke free. He was chasing after me."

"He *what?*" he asked angrily, struggling to get up. I helped pull him up.

"Guard!" Jonathon yelled to him. "Bring Hugo to me *now.*"

"Yes, sir!" He bowed and ran down the hall.

Jonathon was able to catch his breath a couple minutes later. He looked at me.

"I am sorry," I whispered again.

"That was impressive. I just wish it had not happened to me."

We chuckled.

He looked down at my arm, reached up, and stroked it. I looked down and saw Hugo had left marks. I looked back to Jonathon.

"I am going to kill him," he muttered.

Hugo was nowhere to be found.

"How can he just disappear?" King Olov bellowed at some guards. He waved them away angrily. "We finally have a reason to lock him up, and he gets away!" He was pacing in front of his throne.

"I can have a search party sent out," Jonathon suggested.

"No, not yet. I would rather have all the guards here for the engagement ball. We will send some out the morning after."

Jonathon nodded. He looked at me and grabbed my hand, giving it a squeeze. I gave him a weak smile.

A servant approached. "Dinner is ready, Your Majesties." He gave a bow.

We all followed him to the dining room.

Dinner was silent, and none of us ate much. You could stab the stress hanging in the room with one of the forks. King Olov left, followed by the queen. Jonathon and I looked at each other.

He did not let the silence linger.

"If we have twin daughters, let's name one Kate," Jonathon said.

Okay … A little out of the blue, but that is cute that he is thinking about kids already.

"Okay," I responded, smiling. "What about the other one?"

"DupliKate." He just stared at me.

I narrowed my eyes and glared back, and then we both burst out laughing.

"Really? We are not even married yet, and you're already starting in with the dad jokes?"

He shrugged. "I had to lighten the mood. I couldn't take it anymore."

I nodded. "Yeah. What a day, huh?"

"Yeah. I am looking forward to our engagement party tomorrow."

"Me too."

We both smiled.

"Have you thought about what you want for the wedding yet?" he asked.

I shook my head. "I have not. I have been preoccupied with the Hugo mess. You?"

He looked down, put his hands on his chest, and said, "I was thinking about wearing a tux."

I laughed. "That would probably be a good idea." I shook my head. "What is your favorite color?"

"I am a fan of the darker ones: blue, purple, black. What is yours?"

"Blue. It seems like it would be a good idea to make that one of our wedding colors."

"It seems so."

"It will make 'something blue' easy to incorporate." I chuckled.

"For sure." He smiled. "Do you have a favorite cake and frosting flavor?"

"Chocolate and chocolate, hands down. What about you? And do not say vanilla!"

He scrunched his face and shrugged.

"No way!" I said jokingly. "Does it matter if it's the cake or the frosting?"

"Nope!"

"We should probably do vanilla for the frosting. It will go with the white theme of a wedding better."

He nodded. "Chocolate cake with vanilla frosting. Check! What kind of filling?"

"Oh, that will be hard."

"I agree. How about I set up a tasting of fillings soon?"

"That sounds good ... and delicious."

We sat in silence for a minute.

"Shall I escort you back to your room?"

"I would love that."

I found Hanna sitting at the table in my room when I entered. She stood up and curtsied.

"Oh, stop that."

"As you wish."

We smiled.

"We need to find a dress for us for the ball tomorrow," I said.

"To the closet!"

Thankfully, Hanna and I were basically the same size, so she could borrow one of mine. She was more of a girlie girl, so she picked out one of the ones I had refused to wear so far.

It was a strapless dress that came in at the waist and went out into a large, fluffy, gypsy-styled skirt. It was of satin material and pink—all pink, courtesy of Lisette.

"Are you sure I can wear this?"

"Pfft, absolutely! You can even keep the monstrosity."

She squealed in delight.

My eyes fell on another one of Lisette's choices, one that I actually loved.

It was a sleeveless dress. The top was gold with sparkles

covering it. It came in at the waist with a green satin belt, and then the satin continued down into a floor-length, slightly flared skirt. It was beautiful.

We both tried on our dresses, admiring what we saw in the mirror.

"I still can't believe you are getting married."

"I can't either."

"Are you happy?"

"Very much."

We side hugged and stayed that way for a few minutes.

"Well, we should probably take these off and get some rest before tomorrow," I said.

She groaned. "You're probably right." She pouted.

After we changed our clothes, she headed back to her room, while I crawled into bed. My mind flipped back and forth between being excited for tomorrow and terrified about Hugo.

Where was he?

CHAPTER 12

I WAS WOKEN UP BY SOMEONE PLOPPING DOWN ONTO my bed. I opened my eyes and saw Hanna, grinning ear to ear. I could not help but chuckle.

"Yes, Hanna?"

"Get up, sleepyhead! You have an exciting day ahead!"

She went into the bathroom and started my bath.

I sank into the hot water. I was grateful that Hanna was my maid because I did not think I would feel comfortable being naked in front of anyone else.

Once my bath was finished, I got dressed. Even though I was dying to put on the engagement ball gown, I settled on a simpler dress for the first part of the day.

After breakfast, Queen Leona and I double-checked to make sure everything was coming together smoothly. Thankfully, it was. Cooks were bustling around in the kitchen getting the food ready, housekeeping was doing some last-minute cleanup, and other servants were running around getting the decorations put up.

Since there were no other preparations that needed to be done, I headed to the gardens.

It was a beautiful day, not a cloud in the sky. I found an open patch of grass and lay down, soaking up the sun. There was a slight breeze that kept me cool under the hot sun. Birds were singing all around me, and the smell of greenery hung in the air. Other than the nagging reminder that Hugo was still missing, those moments were perfect.

I could feel eyes on me. I opened my own, lifted my head, and looked around.

No one.

I closed my eyes and laid my head back down.

I still felt eyes on me. This time, I sat up and looked around.

"Hello?"

Silence.

I closed my eyes again but stayed sitting up, leaning my head back.

The feeling of being watched never disappeared. Frustrated, I gave up and went back inside.

Lunch was abuzz with talk of the engagement ball. Everyone was talking about visiting family members and the outfits they were going to wear. I, of course, kept mine a secret. I wanted Jonathon to be surprised.

"So, what have you been up to all morning?" I asked Jonathon.

"Last-minute security preparations. We will be ready for any possible attack from Hugo." He smiled.

"Good." I returned the smile.

We went back to eating.

"Would you mind accompanying me in welcoming my aunt, uncle, and Lisette this afternoon?"

"Of course!" I responded. "I am excited to see her again!"

He chuckled. "Good! I know she is excited to see you too."

Lisette and I wrapped each other in a big hug.

"I have missed you!" she said.

"I have missed you too!"

"I know it has only been a couple of weeks but still." She pulled back and held onto my hands. "Mom, Dad? This is Lady Ellena."

"It is wonderful to meet you, dear," her mother said.

"Likewise, ma'am."

Her father held out his hand, and I shook it.

"Let us get you all settled in," King Olov said, motioning for some servants. They got Lisette's family's things and brought them inside.

I brought Lisette into my room to meet Hanna.

"Hi, Hanna! It is so nice to meet you!" Lisette was all smiles.

"Nice to meet you too, Lisette." Hanna gave her a slight bow. Even though she was being polite, I could tell she was being stand-offish to Lisette. I did not blame her. For eighteen years, it was just her and I.

"So, Lisette, what are you going to wear for the ball tonight?" I asked.

"I just bought this red, silky number. It is a halter top that hugs my curves and goes out into a mermaid-style skirt," she said, tracing her silhouette.

"That will look beautiful on you," I said.

"I know. Thank you," she replied, smiling.

Hanna lifted an eyebrow at me with her comment. I knew she took it as cocky. After getting to know Lisette though, I took it as confident.

I shook my head, grinning.

"What are you guys going to wear?" Lisette inquired.

I proceeded to tell her about our outfits.

"Oh, you guys are going to look lovely!"

"Thank you," I said.

Hanna remained silent. I nudged her.

"Yes, thank you."

Thank heavens Lisette seemed oblivious to Hanna's attitude.

"Well, girls, I am going to go soak in the tub before getting ready. I will see you tonight!" She bounced out of my room.

I looked at Hanna.

"She seems … nice."

I rolled my eyes, smacking her arm. "Come on. Let's get you ready first."

After Hanna was dressed, she sat down at the vanity, and I got to work on her hair. I curled it and then put it up, leaving some tendrils down to frame her face.

"You look beautiful," I said, resting my hands on her shoulders.

"Thank you. I feel like it!" she replied, resting her hands on mine. "Okay, your turn!"

I put my dress on and took her spot at the vanity.

"I have not seen you do waves yet. Are you okay if I do that?" Hanna asked.

"Wave away!"

After she took a wave iron to my hair, she took small patches from each side, twisted them, and brought them together in the back.

"Thank you, Hanna. I feel like a princess!"

"Good, because you will be soon enough."

We sat in silence for a moment, soaking in that sentence.

"So, are you going to the ball with anyone special?" I asked.

"Maybe …"

"Do I know him?"

"Yep!"

"Who is it?"

She stared at me, starting to blush.

"Come on, Hanna. Who?"

"Thomas."

What?

"Are you serious? We have known him for *years*, and you never seemed to like him that way!"

"I didn't, but he has been bulking up and getting tan since becoming a stable boy." She looked down. "He also told me that he has liked me for years."

I jumped up. "What?"

I pulled her into a hug. "Hanna, that's awesome!"

"I know, right? Apparently, him seeing me with other guys made him brave enough to make a move."

I could not stop smiling. "Wait. How is he going to be at the ball?"

"He is making our own private dance floor in the stables. The music will be plenty loud, and I am going to snag us some food and drinks."

"Aw, that is so cute!"

"I know!"

"Well, I will not keep you from Thomas. Go to him. Jonathon will be stopping by soon anyway to get me."

We hugged, and she left.

I did not have to wait long before there was a knock on my door.

I opened it to see him wearing a black tuxedo with glossy lapels, a gold handkerchief sticking out of the pocket, and no tie, with the top button undone.

Dear heavens.

We both stood there, staring at the other.

I cleared my throat. "You look incredible tonight."

He stopped looking me up and down and met my eyes. "Thank you. You do too."

I took his outstretched arm, and we headed toward the staircase.

We paused when we reached the top, the noisy ball drifting up to us. I took a deep breath. He took my hand, interlocking our fingers. We began our descent.

There was a brief moment of silence before the room broke out into thunderous applause. We smiled and waved to everyone. Jonathon held up his hand to quiet everyone.

"We would like to thank everyone for being here to celebrate this evening with us."

He looked down at me. We smiled at each other.

"We cannot wait to set a date and will let you all know when we do. For tonight, please enjoy yourselves!"

The applause started up again. We joined the king and queen on their stage.

"You look beautiful, my dear," Queen Leona said.

"Thank you, Your Majesty. So do you."

She gave me slight bow.

"Yes, Lady Ellena, you look wonderful this evening. You and Jonathon make a perfect couple." He put his arm around Jonathon.

I gave him a curtsy.

"Thank you, Father," Jonathon said, wrapping his other arm around the king.

The music stopped, and the crowd parted, making a circle in the middle of the room with a path leading from it to us. Jonathon looked down at me.

"May I have this dance?" he asked, pulling my hand up to his lips.

"Yes, you may." I curtsied in response.

He led me to the middle of the circle. The music started again, this time playing a song with a slower tempo. Thank heavens I remembered the steps from the first ball we danced at. I looked up at him.

"No traveling." I squinted my eyes at him.

He laughed. "No traveling." He spun me out. The crowd clapped.

I groaned as he pulled me back in.

"What is wrong?" he asked.

"I hate being stared at," I whispered.

He chuckled. "Are you sure you want to marry me?"

"I am sure. You are worth putting up with it for."

His eyes shined as he smiled.

We continued dancing until the song came to an end and Jonathon dipped me. The crowd cheered. He pulled me up.

"Ready to hide for a little bit?" he asked.

"Yes, please!"

We headed to one of the food tables and grabbed some refreshments.

"You and my mom did a wonderful job picking out this delicious spread."

"Thank you. I have enjoyed getting to know her better lately."

"She has too."

Yes.

We munched on our food for a few minutes.

"Does your father like me?"

Jonathon looked at me. "Very much so. I know he does not show his emotions often, but he has talked about how much he likes you."

I let out a breath of relief.

Double yes.

Someone hugged me from behind. I turned to see Lisette.

"You look gorgeous!" she said, pulling back, looking at me.

"Thank you! So do you!" I may have been the future princess

of Olandia, but more eyes would be on her tonight. I did not mind that one bit.

"I will leave you ladies to it. I have my own rounds to make." We kissed, and I watched him disappear into the crowd.

Lisette and I talked for a while before an upbeat song began playing.

"Oh! We have to dance to this!" Lisette said, grabbing my hand and pulling me farther onto the floor.

I swayed to the beat, while she moved her body in ways I never had. I was right about the other eyes in the room. Girls gave her admiring, sometimes jealous looks, while the men gave her a whole other look.

I admired her confidence. Would I ever feel that comfortable in front of other people? I guessed only time would tell.

The song ended, and I excused myself from Lisette's presence. I had to peek in on Hanna.

I walked through the kitchen and exited through the open door in the back. I proceeded quietly to the stables.

I crouched down as I approached and peered into a window. There were candles everywhere, giving the stable a romantic air. In the middle of the aisle were Hanna and Thomas, swaying together in each other's arms.

"Good for you, Hanna," I whispered, watching them a few seconds more before heading back toward the castle.

I heard the crunch of the pebbles on the ground behind me. I turned my head and saw… Hugo. I turned back around and picked up my pace.

I peeked behind me and saw that he did not pick up his own.

I hurried into the kitchen door, where I was met by two guards standing inside.

Thank heavens.

"I have just seen Hugo. He is right through there." I pointed to the doors just as Hugo stepped in, eerily calm.

I turned to the guards. They did not move to apprehend him.

"What are you waiting for? Arrest him!"

Hugo chuckled.

I turned to face him.

"Dear Lady Ellena. They do not answer to you." He looked at them and nodded toward me. Before I could blink, they had me by both arms.

No!

Hugo approached me. "There is a reason why I was able to escape that day. I have most of these men on my payroll."

This cannot be!

He stroked my face with his hand. I nipped at it. He withdrew it quickly, laughing.

"I love that fire. Keep it. You are going to need it."

I pushed back against the two guards, ramming them into the counter behind us. Wine bottles went crashing onto the floor, chardonnay going everywhere. Their grip on me did not loosen. I opened my mouth to yell, but one of them clamped their hand across it. I bit down hard. He yelped and pulled it back. I tried to wriggle free, but it was no use. They were bigger and stronger. I went to yell again. A hand came up to my mouth again, but this time, it held a wet cloth firmly against my face. After a couple more seconds of struggling, everything went black.

CHAPTER 13

I SAT UP STRAIGHT, BREATHING HEAVILY.

I was in a bed but not mine. It was smaller, like the size of a twin, and only had a single blanket on it. I looked around. I was in a room that was sectioned off by a set of bars. My side was smaller. I had no windows on my side, just the bed. The room allowed for some walking space but not much.

I looked through the bars into the other side of the room. It had a poorly thrown together living room with only a love seat and television. In the corner was a door to a small room—a restroom maybe? In the middle of the room was a set of stairs. It appeared as if I was in a basement.

I was alone. I jumped out of the bed and started running to each bar, shaking them violently, seeing if any were loose.

Nope.

The door would not even budge. I smacked it and cursed. I brought my hands to the sides of my face and tried to think of a way out of there.

The door at the top of the stairs opened. I spun around to see Hugo coming down them. I grabbed onto the bars and glared at him.

"Ah. You're awake." He stopped halfway across the room, smiling at me. My stomach tightened.

"Let me out," I growled at him.

He puckered his lips at me. "I am sorry, but I can't. I kind of need you."

I grimaced. "You are going to regret this."

He breathed in loudly. "I may, but I don't think so."

"What makes you so sure?"

"Because I have been planning and recruiting for *years*. I have been waiting for the perfect time, and it has come."

"Why now?"

"Because of you, my dear. The royal family *and* the country have been preoccupied with the future princess of Olandia. So, thank you." He grinned evilly.

I let go of the bars.

Was the king going to get hurt because of me?

The thought made me sick.

Hugo's phone rang. He picked up, groaned an acknowledgment, and hung up. He went to the television and turned it on.

There was the royal family, at a podium, with a scrolling marquee on the bottom, saying: "Emergency! Lady Ellena, the future princess of Olandia, has been abducted." I pressed my face against the bars, holding tight to them.

Jonathon.

He looked like he had not slept all night. His eyes were pink with bags under them, and his hair was not neatly combed like it usually was.

How long have I been gone?

King Olov stepped up to the mic.

"We noticed Lady Ellena missing around nine o'clock last night."

Thank heavens, it has not been too long.

"There appears to have been a struggle in the kitchen."

I could see Jonathon shift on his feet behind his father.

"Based on past experiences, we believe that Hugo Ossler is behind the abduction."

Gasps erupted from the crowd.

"If anyone has any information on his whereabouts, do not hesitate to call the police."

He stepped away from the mic, and Jonathon stepped up. My heart sped up.

"I second what my father has said: do not be afraid to contact the authorities if you have even an inkling of where he could be. We believe him to be behind not only this abduction but the past attempts on my father's life as well. He is an enemy of Olandia and must be brought to justice."

His eyes went from a determined look to a more softened look, staring straight into the camera.

"Ellena."

I could feel tears forming in my eyes.

"I *will* find you."

He stepped away from the mic, off the podium, and into the castle.

Jonathon.

I closed my eyes, and the tears threatened to fall. Hugo turned off the television.

"Whew! What a moving broadcast. I was *almost* scared!" He chuckled.

My eyes shot open. I bore all my hate toward him through my glare.

He turned his head. "Don't be like that. I will let you use the restroom a few times a day, and you'll get three square meals! Speaking of which, here is your breakfast."

He walked over with a tray full of food.

When he got close enough, I smacked the tray up into his face.

He shook the food off. "Very well. No food for today."

He turned around, went up the stairs, and slammed the door shut.

I collapsed onto the ground. I could not stop the crying fit that ensued.

I must have been there a while because my bottom leg had fallen asleep. The door at the top of the stairs opened, and a man I had never seen before came down.

I pulled myself up with the bars. He came to my door and opened it.

"Don't try anything funny," he commanded.

He led me to the room in the corner. "Three minutes."

I entered the tiny half bathroom. There was a sink directly across from the door and a toilet right next to it.

As I was doing my business, I looked around the room, seeing if there was a way out. There was not—no window and no oversized air duct.

There was a knock on the door. "Time's up."

He took me back to my cage, locked the door, and disappeared up the stairs.

My stomach growled. I crawled into the bed, hoping to sleep away the intense hunger I now felt in my stomach and the aching in my heart for Jonathon.

I woke up to Hugo clanging on the bars. He held a tray of steaming hot, delicious-smelling food. I sat up.

"You can have this, *if* you are going to play nice."

I nodded.

He opened my door and came inside, placing the tray next to me. I looked at him for a moment before diving into the food. There were hot scrambled eggs, crispy toast, crunchy bacon, and fresh fruit. I could not eat it fast enough.

Hugo was staring at me.

"What do you want?" I asked, shoveling another bite of food in.

"Do you know why I am doing it?"

I looked at him and shrugged. "You dislike the way King Olov runs the country."

He chuckled. "It's more than that. I believe that I can do *better*."

I stared at him. "What makes you think that?"

"Because I will return things to the way they should be. Class lines are becoming blurred; they need to stay distinct. We are appearing weak to other countries by always trying to avoid conflict. We need them to fear us."

"Has it ever crossed your mind that nonviolent solutions are a smart way to go? No one has to die, from *either* side. It opens doors for future trade and the like."

He laughed.

"One does not truly obtain unless it is by force."

It was my turn to laugh. "That is insane. You are not obtaining if it is by force. You are stealing. You are truly obtaining if the other is giving it up freely."

He looked me up and down. "And what if they are not willing to give it up?"

I stood up. "Then you do not take it." I stared him down, clenching my fists at my side.

He stood up. I backed up.

He smirked, gathered up the rest of the food, and left.

I let out a breath I did not realize I had been holding.

I need to get out of here.

CHAPTER 14

JUST LIKE HE SAID, I WAS BROUGHT LUNCH AND DINner and allowed to use the restroom before bed. Thankfully, Hugo did not visit me again the rest of the day.

I searched around my room.

My bed was welded metal, so there were no pieces that could be taken off. There was no light on my side, so I could not make anything out of its pieces. He took my shoes so I could not use my heels as a weapon. Hugo was thorough.

Dang it.

I fell back onto my bed in frustration.

Ouch!

Something sharp poked my head. I put my hand up and searched around. Nestled in my hair was a bobby pin.

I breathed a sigh of relief.

Thank you, Hanna.

I ran to my door and placed the bobby pin inside the lock. I fumbled around for a few minutes before it clicked open.

Yes!

I took off the lock and opened the door. I put the pin back into my hair and walked to the bottom of the stairs. I took a deep breath and slowly made my way to the top.

I put my ear to the door.

Nothing.

I turned the knob and slowly opened the door.

No lights were on. I peeked my head out. There did not seem to be anyone around. I proceeded onto the next floor. There was a window right in front of me. We were surrounded by trees. I saw a building off in the distance. I squinted as I walked closer to the window.

The castle. I could see it! It was either foolish that he held me there, in direct view of the castle, or brilliant, if the royal family thought he would hide far away.

I heard a creak above me from the second floor. I spun around, shut the door quietly, and ran down the stairs. I booked it back to my room, shut and locked the gate, and sat down on my bed. I tried to slow my breathing in case someone came down. Thankfully, no one did.

I brought my hands to my head and chuckled. I could not believe I had a way out of there! I was planning on doing reconnaissance again tomorrow night. Hopefully, I would get farther than I did tonight.

Hugo came down with breakfast again the next morning. I ate like a lady.

"I am going to move forward to the next phase tonight," he said.

I looked at him. "And what does that entail?"

"Finally killing King Olov." He grinned.

"You have tried and failed twice before. What makes you think you will be successful this time?"

His smile faded. "Because there is no way it can fail this time. The guard stationed outside of his room will go in and stab him in the heart while he sleeps tonight." His grin returned.

My heart dropped. No one would see. No one would hear. No one would know until the morning when it would be too late.

Panic set in. I had to get out tonight. I had to make it back to the palace and warn King Olov.

I stopped eating. I was not hungry anymore.

"Does this upset you?" he asked mockingly.

I glared at him.

"Would you like to know the rest of my plan?"

I did not answer.

"Once King Olov is *disposed* of, Jonathon will assume the throne. I will then come to an arrangement with him. No harm will come to you as long as he complies with my demands."

"What demands?"

"All the things I told you yesterday—distinct class lines and resolutions with more power behind them."

I shifted on the bed.

"Brilliant, isn't it? If he cares for you as much as I believe he does, he will not put up a fight."

My breath quickened. "Why don't you just kill the whole royal family and take over by force?"

"Because the people would immediately reject me. I would get nowhere."

As much as I hated to admit it, his plan was diabolically brilliant.

I have to get out of here. Tonight.

CHAPTER 15

Jonathon

IT HAS BEEN THE LONGEST TWO DAYS OF MY LIFE. I have not slept, and except for the occasional nibble of food, I have not eaten. I failed Ellena.

She was with a man who, until recently, I did not believe was capable of such acts of violence. However, he had proven me wrong, and I was terrified of what he was doing to Ellena.

My heartbeat picked up, and my breathing quickened. I clenched my fists.

I will find him, and when I do, I will kill him.

There was a knock on my door.

"Enter."

"Your father requests your presence. There have been new developments in Lady Ellena's disappearance."

I bolted out my door and to my father's office.

I threw open his door. "What is it, Father?"

"We have received an anonymous tip that he is hiding out in the forest to the west of us. I have sent out a small scouting group. We will know if it is a lead worth pursuing in the hour."

Please, God, let it be them.

I could not just sit there waiting for the report. I had to keep myself busy, or I was going to go crazy.

"Excuse me, Father." I bowed and left.

I walked to the room that would become Ellena's and mine once we were married. It was easy for me to picture her in there. I could see her standing in front of the open balcony doors, the wind softly blowing her hair and dress. I could see her sitting in one of the armchairs, reading a book. I could see her peaceful face, asleep in the bed.

I brought my hand up to my chest. My heart ached. I did not think it was possible to care for someone that much that fast, but from the moment I saw her, I was drawn to her.

First, it was her beauty. Then it was her smile and the way she would look away when she was embarrassed. Those eyes. I have never seen eyes that shade of green. Her hair. The color reminded me of the color of a wet beach, one of my favorite places to be. I also could not get enough of her laugh. I would go to any length to hear it.

I went out onto the balcony and looked out into the forest to the west of us.

Where are you, Ellena?

There was still so much that I wanted to learn about her. I knew she hated the dark, but what else did she fear? Besides books, what else were her interests? What were her insecurities? What did she believe were her strengths? What was it like growing up in an orphanage? How many children did she want? These were all questions that I wanted to spend the rest of my life finding out.

I left the room and started walking around the halls. There were portraits of my family and ancestors scattered throughout the castle. I could not wait to have one of Ellena up there too, to immortalize her for future generations.

A guard came panting around the corner.

"Your Highness." He bowed, and I returned the gesture. "We have found Hugo."

I put my hand on his shoulder. "Thank you." I took off running back to my father's office.

He was already surrounded by servants, dressing him up in bulletproof gear. "Suit up, son. It is time to kill that treasonous, pathetic excuse of a man."

CHAPTER 16

Ellena

I ONLY WAITED A COUPLE OF MINUTES AFTER THEY left with the dinner tray before I fumbled the lock open again. There was no way I would have a chance of making it out if I went the same way as yesterday. So I pushed the love seat under one of the windows and climbed up on it. The window opened with ease. I pushed the screen out and stuck my head out, looking around.

No one.

I pulled myself up and out of the window. I shimmied along the house until I came to one of the corners that faced the castle in the distance. I peeked around. There was one man with a dog heading the other way. I waited until they disappeared around the other corner. I took a step.

"Snap!" A twig echoed out from under my foot.

Oh sh—

"Woof woof!"

I took off running. I was barefoot and in a floor-length gown, and it was proving to be very difficult.

After dodging a few trees, I was tackled from behind and slammed into the ground face-first. A large, snarling dog stood on top of me, barking and drooling.

A whistle called the dog off. Within seconds, someone yanked me up by my arm. It was the man who accompanied the dog. I heard clapping from behind me. I turned and saw Hugo approaching, smiling.

"I am impressed, Lady Ellena. You *almost* made it—what?" He looked back to the house and then to where I stood again. "Twenty feet?" He laughed.

I spat at his feet. He dodged it.

He grabbed me by my dress straps and pulled me close.

"I will teach you to show me more respect." He pulled me into a hard kiss.

Yuck!

"Hugo!" a familiar voice boomed from the side.

I pushed Hugo off me and turned.

Jonathon.

He was standing a little way away with a gun pointed at Hugo. Within moments, Hugo pulled me into his arm, facing Jonathon, with a gun to my head.

"Don't do anything stupid, Jonathon." He pressed it into my temple.

Jonathon's face was full of fear and confusion. He looked at me.

I closed my eyes, elbowed Hugo as hard as I could in his gut, then jumped to the side. He immediately floundered, and Jonathon took his shot. He got Hugo in the shoulder. Hugo grabbed his wounded shoulder and took off running, with Jonathon close behind him.

People came pouring out of the house as guards and King Olov appeared from the same direction that Jonathon had come. Shots fired from all directions.

I ducked and ran behind a bush. I knew Jonathon would want me to run back to the castle, but I could not abandon him there.

I ran in a crouch toward the direction I saw Hugo and Jonathon go. I found them running through the trees, shooting at each other. Jonathon must have run out of bullets because he threw his gun down and pounced onto Hugo from behind. Hugo's gun went sliding away. I ran toward it.

I made it to the gun and picked it up.

"Shoot him!" Jonathon yelled. But they were wrestling so much that I did not feel comfortable taking the shot. Hugo wrapped his hands around Jonathon's neck. He struggled in his grasp. I took a deep breath, steadied the gun, and shot at Hugo's head.

Everything went silent for a moment. I could only hear my own heavy breathing. A couple of seconds later, I could hear Jonathon's breathing join mine and watched as Hugo's hands fell to the ground.

I breathed a sigh of relief and let the gun drop to the ground.

Jonathon immediately jumped up and ran over to me, pulling me into his arms. I collapsed into his arms and started crying.

"Shh, I've got you." He stroked my back.

"I was scared that I would never see you again," I whispered.

He bent down and lifted my head to look at him. "I told you that I would find you." He smiled.

I pulled him into a desperate kiss.

An engine roared nearby. We pulled apart and turned to see a jeep driving toward the other conflict. We looked at each other, grabbed the other's hand, and ran, following the jeep.

It started plowing through the crowd of palace guards. It was a horrible sight. One of them fired a shot into the windshield, hitting the driver, causing the jeep to swerve uncontrollably.

The same time that it crashed into the tree, we heard a loud scream. We ran toward it. There, pinned between the jeep and the tree, was King Olov.

CHAPTER 17

"NO!" JONATHON YELLED AS HE RAN TO HIS FATHER.

My hands flew to my mouth as I walked over, stunned.

King Olov was lying on the hood of the jeep, his breathing ragged. He was holding Jonathon's hand. "I am so proud of you, my boy," he told his son.

"Thank you, Father." He stroked the king's hand.

"You are going to make a wonderful king." He was now whispering.

"And you." He looked at me. "Are going to make a wonderful queen and wife." He gave me a weak smile.

"Thank you," I whispered, trying to smile, tears falling.

He looked back to his son, one last time, before all light vanished from his eyes. Jonathon reached over and closed them.

Jonathon stood up straight and turned to the rest of us.

"I need you to move the jeep. I need you two to bring a stretcher. And I need you to help me carry the king back," Jonathon commanded some guards.

After his directions were hastily followed, we made our way back to the castle. Thankfully, no guards lost their lives, but several of them were wounded. I walked alongside one, holding him up as he hobbled on his good leg.

We all entered the long driveway to the castle. Queen Leona came out the front doors. She smiled when she saw Jonathon was safe. She scanned over the rest of us. When her eyes fell on the stretcher behind her son, she screamed and ran down to it.

We all stopped. She collapsed onto her husband and wept loudly.

"Come on, Mom," Jonathon whispered, handing the stretcher to another guard and wrapping his arm around his mother.

Jonathon and his mother disappeared onto the third floor, while I helped get the wounded to the hospital wing. King Olov's body was laid on a bed and covered with a white sheet.

I did not want to interrupt Jonathon and his mother, so I paced back and forth across the main hall.

"Ellena!"

I turned and saw Hanna running toward me. She collided into me, and we held each other tight, both of us crying.

"Thank God you are okay!" she said through tears.

I nodded. "I am fine, but … King Olov is dead, Hanna."

She pulled away. "No …"

I didn't want to believe it either.

I nodded again, looking down.

We stood in silence for several moments.

I heard footsteps echoing through the main hall. I looked up and saw Jonathon making his way over.

Hanna hugged me one more time and made her exit.

Jonathon stopped just in front of me, his hands in his pockets, looking at the ground. I did not know what to say, so I stayed silent, joining his gaze at the floor.

"Thank you for coming to get me," I finally managed to get out.

He pulled me into a tight hug. I held onto his torso, feeling him take deep, shaky breaths.

"I thought I was going to lose you," he whispered.

I looked up at him. "Never." I gave him a weak smile.

He stroked my cheek, staring deeply into my eyes. "I love you, Ellena."

Tears filled my eyes. "I love you too, Jonathon." I pulled him into a deep kiss. Our hands roamed each other's face and body as our lips moved heatedly against each other.

We pulled away breathless. He leaned his forehead on mine.

"Be with me." I pulled back and looked at him, surprised. I searched his eyes.

I put my hand onto his cheek. "As much as I want to …" *And I want to* … "We should wait until it can be just you and me—not you, me, your father, and Hugo." I smiled.

He turned into my hand and kissed it. "You are right." He smiled back.

At sunset, a week later, King Olov's family gathered on his favorite cliff. Queen Leona and Jonathon were at the edge, with Lisette, her parents, and me behind them.

They had an arm around each other as they looked out over the ocean. They reached into the jar and opened their hands, letting the wind carry away King Olov's ashes.

After the urn was emptied, Jonathon came back to the rest of us and put his arm around me. We all turned around and walked back to the castle, leaving Queen Leona alone.

I ate very little at dinner, alone. Queen Leona stayed in her room, and Jonathon said he was going for a walk in the garden. Having given him time, I decided to go look for him.

I found him at the bench by the fountain, staring at the water. I joined him and put my hand on his leg. He put his hand on top of mine.

We sat in silence for a moment.

"My father is gone, Ellena." He choked back a cry.

"You know, it's okay to cry."

He shook his head. "A good king does not cry."

"Maybe … but you are not king yet. And you will be more than a good king; you will be a great one."

With that, he turned and wrapped me into a hug, crying into my shoulder. I held him close, rubbing his back.

I did not say anything. I simply held him and let him release all that he needed to.

A little while later, his head was in my lap, looking up at me. I stroked his hair, looking down at him.

"Thank you, Ellena."

"You're welcome."

He pulled my head down for a kiss.

He looked at his watch and sat up. "It's past midnight. We should head to bed. Because today, whether I like it or not, I become king."

CHAPTER 18

QUEEN LEONA SAT IN THE FRONT ROW, NEXT TO THE aisle. I was right beside her, with Lisette and her family directly behind us.

The archbishop stood. "We have mourned the loss of our beloved King Olov. May he rest in peace." The congregation bowed and echoed the last part.

He continued. "Our beloved country cannot remain without a king. Our dear Prince Jonathon has agreed to take his father's place, starting today." He motioned to the back of the room.

We all turned and watched as Jonathon regally walked the aisle up to the archbishop.

He turned, faced the congregation, and kneeled. The archbishop placed an orb in his left hand and a scepter in his right. He then stood behind Jonathon, hovering the crown above his head.

"Do you, Jonathon Larsson, swear to rule Olandia, according to her laws, with justice and mercy?"

"I, Jonathon Larsson, do swear to rule Olandia, according to her laws, with justice and mercy."

"Do you swear to protect her from all threats, both foreign and domestic?"

"I do swear to protect her from all threats, both foreign and domestic."

"Do you swear to do all these things until your dying day?"

"I do swear to do all these things until my dying day."

With this, the archbishop lowered the crown onto Jonathon's head.

He placed himself beside Jonathon. "I present to you, Olandia, your king. King Jonathon Larsson."

Jonathon rose proudly as the congregation stood and burst into cheers.

He looked down at me and smiled. I smiled back, tears hanging in my eyes.

I am so proud of you.

We celebrated with the traditional garden party. Even though there was a sadness that hung in the air from King Olov's death, everyone was excited for Jonathon's rule.

Jonathon was busy making his rounds to members of parliament, so I joined Queen Leona at her usual table outside.

"Everyone has high hopes for Jonathon," I said, watching him from across the lawn.

She smiled. "They should. He will do a wonderful job."

"Yes, he will."

We sat there silently for a few minutes.

"I am sorry about your husband," I whispered, looking down.

She looked down too. "Thank you. He died fighting for something he believed in and for someone that he believed would make a great future queen."

We looked at each other.

"Thank you." Tears were welling up in my eyes.

"It's true. You have shown us that you are hardworking, brave, and kind to those in a lower station. I can't wait to see what you do as queen." She put her hand on mine.

I put my other hand on top of hers. "What will happen to you when I become queen?"

"I get to be released of all of the responsibilities that come with the title, while still reaping the benefits of it."

We laughed.

"May I come to you when I have questions? I know I am going to have many."

"Absolutely."

"Great."

A throat cleared near us. We looked up and saw Jonathon approaching.

"May I have a word with Lady Ellena, Mother?"

"She is all yours," she said, releasing my hands.

I stood and walked beside Jonathon as we made our way around the gardens.

"How are you enjoying the party, *King* Jonathon?"

He chuckled. "I have had everyone call me that all afternoon, but it still sounds foreign to me."

"I am sure that it takes some getting used to, especially when you were not expecting it this soon."

"Yeah ..."

We walked in silence.

"I know our courtship was really short, and I was hoping to give you a longer engagement because of it."

We stopped and looked at each other.

"But I can't be a king without you by my side."

"But I thought Olandian law didn't require a queen for a king to rule," I said, confused.

He shook his head, smiling. "It doesn't. I don't *want* to rule without you."

Oh...

I smiled back. "I don't need a long engagement. We will have the rest of our lives to get to know each other more."

He took my hands in his and rubbed my knuckles.

"So ... when were you thinking?" I asked.

"How does next week sound?"

CHAPTER 19

SINCE LISETTE WAS STILL IN TOWN, I DECIDED TO DO MY wedding dress shopping the next day. I took both her and Hanna with me to Belle's Boutique.

Lisette brought out a huge, fluffy number.

"Absolutely not!" I said.

"Oh, come on. Why not?" she asked.

"I don't feel like walking down the aisle as a marshmallow!"

Hanna chuckled from a nearby bench. "Let me try."

She came back with a form-fitting, satin dress with a low-cut front and back.

"Dang, Hanna! That would leave nothing to the imagination!"

"I find it tastefully revealing," she said.

I raised an eyebrow. "How about we let me try."

I looked around for a few minutes and found the perfect dress.

"Close your eyes!" I told Hanna and Lisette.

They obeyed, and I ran into the dressing room with my pick. I put it on.

It was me. It was a strapless, floor-length, satin gown underneath a lace layer that covered the exposed parts of my chest, shoulders, back, and arms down to my wrist. I walked out of the dressing room.

"Okay ... Open them."

They both opened their eyes and gasped.

"Ellena, that is perfect!" Hanna said.

"It really is," Lisette agreed.

"Thanks. I think so too." I turned back to the mirror and admired the dress.

Lisette came over and added a veil that went down to my waist.

We all stared into the mirror and smiled.

The next day, Jonathon wrapped a blindfold around my eyes and led me up what felt like three flights of stairs.

"What in the world? Where did the extra flight of stairs come from?"

He chuckled. "You'll see."

A moment later, we stopped, and he removed the blindfold. We were on the roof of the castle. It was a beautiful, cloudy day.

There were two chairs and a little table that was covered by various cakes with filling samples.

I could not hide my smile.

He pulled out my chair, and I took it.

He picked up a plate with two bites on it. "The first is our chocolate cake with vanilla frosting and strawberry filling." He picked one up and headed toward my mouth. I opened and let him put it in.

"Mmmm," I said.

He put the other piece in his mouth. "Mm. That is good." He put the plate down. "Your pick."

I looked across the table and picked up one with a label by it that read, "Blueberry filling."

I picked up a piece and placed it into his open mouth, then put one in mine.

He stared at me. "What do you think?"

"I don't think it meshes well with the other flavors."

"I agree."

I put the plate down, and he picked up the one with cherry filling.

"Oh, that one is my favorite!" I said, after sampling my piece.

"Same here. It is very reminiscent of a chocolate-covered cherry."

"It totally is!"

As I went to pick up the next plate, I felt a drop on my hand, then another and another. I looked up at the sky. The clouds were releasing their retained water.

I closed my eyes and soaked in the feeling. I loved the rain.

"You know, I have not had the pleasure of dancing with you alone yet," Jonathon stated.

I opened my eyes and saw that he was standing by me with his hand held out.

I took it, and he pulled me to my feet.

We walked away from the table to give ourselves space. He pulled me in close. We started dancing to the tempo of the raindrops, which were slow and melodic.

We stared at each other as the rain continued to fall around us. It had soaked his hair to the point that it was starting to drip off it. One drop fell onto my face.

He released my hand that he was holding and wiped it off, not that it made a difference; my face was soaked. The gesture was still romantic.

He pulled me into a kiss.

As I went to move my hands onto him, a crack of thunder made us jump.

"Maybe we should get inside," he said as he led us back into the castle.

I was in the main hall the next day, picking out our wedding reception décor, when a guard approached me.

"Lady Ellena, King Jonathon requests your presence."

"Lead the way."

I was shocked when he led me to a room on the second floor.

The meeting floor?

Jonathon was standing at the front of a long table with all the members of parliament sitting around it.

"Lady Ellena." He gave me a bow. I curtsied back.

He gave an *ahem* to the rest of the room, and they all nodded their heads in bows. I returned them.

He pointed to a chair next to him, along the long side of the table. I took it.

"Why am I here, King Jonathon?" I inquired.

"I am in need of your opinion on a very important matter. How do we address the civil unrest in the kingdom?"

Several voices around the room showed their opposition at him asking for my advice.

Jonathon held up his hand to hush them.

"She is my future wife and your future queen, and I, your king, have requested her voice on the matter."

He looked back to me. "Go on, Lady Ellena."

I took a deep breath. "I believe that the first thing we need to do is address your safety, Your Majesty, by firing all of the current guards and hiring new ones. When I was captured by Hugo, he told me how a lot of the guards were on his payroll."

Gasps broke out around the room.

Jonathon nodded. "We will do that immediately. Anything else, Lady Ellena?"

"Although I do not agree with the violent measures Hugo and his men took, I wonder if they felt unheard. What if we were to start hearing the people more?"

He sat down in his seat and stroked his chin, taking my words seriously. "How would we go about doing that?"

"We could create a council that would receive all the people's grievances. The council members would address the smaller issues themselves, while the bigger ones would be directed to you."

"To us," he corrected.

I smiled. "To us."

He nodded and stood. "I like it. What say you, members of parliament?"

There was a very long moment of silence as I stared down at the table.

"Let's do it," "I like it," "Aye," the voices rose up in affirmation.

I let out a breath that I did not know I was holding. I looked up and found Jonathon smiling down at me.

He leaned down and whispered into my ear. "You are going to make a wonderful queen."

My wedding was quickly approaching, and I had not set up my side of the bridal party yet.

I found Hanna first. She was eating lunch with Thomas in the kitchen.

"Hey, Thomas. Can I borrow Hanna?"

"Sure, Ellena. Sorry! I mean Lady Ellena."

"Please. We knew each other way before all of this. You can just call me Ellena." I gave him a smile and led Hanna into the hall.

"What's up?" she asked.

"You know you are my best friend. So … you should also know that there is no one else that I would rather ask to be my maid of honor."

She started jumping up and down squealing. "I was wondering when you were finally going to ask me! Cutting it a little close, aren't you?" She nudged me.

"Hey! In case you haven't noticed, it has been a little chaotic around her lately." I nudged her back.

"I know. What dress do you have in mind? Are you going to do the typical *ugly bridesmaid dresses so you look good* thing?"

I laughed. "No. You can have your choice of dress. It just has to be navy blue." I smiled.

"Yes!" She gave me a hug and ran back into the kitchen. I could overhear her saying to Thomas, "We are going shopping!"

I found Lisette next. Because of everything happening with King Olov, Jonathon, and I, her family had decided to stay through the wedding.

"Would you mind doing me the honor of being my bridesmaid?"

"Absolutely!" She pulled me into a hug. She pulled back just as quickly. "Can I help plan your bridal shower?"

"You will have to ask Hanna, but *I* have no problem with it," I replied, smiling.

She clapped her hands together excitedly. "I will be right back!"

She took off down the hall. She was back in just a couple of minutes.

She was smiling widely. "She agreed, as long as she was the main planner of it. I told her I was fine with that as long as there was *plenty* of alcohol."

Uh oh.

A couple of days later, Hanna and Lisette ambushed me in the dining room after dinner.

"Excuse us, Your Majesties, but we must borrow Lady Ellena for the evening," Lisette said sweetly.

Queen Leona giggled, and Jonathon got up, came over, and gave me a kiss.

"Bring her back in one piece, *Lisette*." He raised an eyebrow at her.

She laughed. "Don't worry, cousin. She *should* still be able to marry you tomorrow."

He shook his head, smiling, as they dragged me away.

There was a limo waiting outside for us.

Yes!

"Ta da!" Hanna said, throwing out her arms.

I could not hide my huge grin.

Lisette opened the door, crawled in, and came back out holding a bottle of champagne. She handed us each a glass, then filled them up.

We all chugged our drinks.

"That's what I'm talking about!" Lisette said, filling our glasses again.

We all giggled and crawled in.

"To our destination, please!" Hanna called out to the driver.

We all downed another glass on the drive over.

We stopped at a cliff that overlooked an empty lake and got out. There was a zipline that went across it.

"Um, Hanna? You remember I hate heights, right?"

"That's what this is for!" she answered, pouring me another glass.

It's called liquid courage, right?

Instead of drinking from my glass, I grabbed the bottle from her and took a long swig. Her and Lisette laughed.

"All right. Let's do this!" I yelled.

Hanna and Lisette cheered next to me.

I got myself strapped in and gripped the cord for dear life, squinting my eyes shut.

"Ready?" Hanna asked.

All I could do was nod. With that, I was off.

I could feel the wind rushing past me. Maybe it was the alcohol, maybe not, but I had the courage to open my eyes.

The view was incredible! The lake was surrounded by acres of deciduous trees that were a brilliant green. The water was crystal clear beneath me.

I could not help myself; I started to laugh. This was thrilling! I let out a yell as I reached the end.

I came to an abrupt stop and hopped down. I walked to the edge of the lake and looked up at the cliff to see Lisette strapping herself in.

She sped down gleefully, followed by Hanna.

Once she reached the bottom, we made our trek back up to the cliff.

We sat down a little way away from the edge and talked for a while. Hanna and I shared stories about growing up in the orphanage, and Lisette shared what it had been like growing up related to the royal family.

Hanna stood up. "There is one more thing that we need to do before we leave."

I watched her walk to the edge and turn back to us. "We are going to jump!"

Say what now?

Lisette and I looked at each other and then joined Hanna. We peered over the edge.

I looked at Hanna. "It turns out Jonathon should have been more afraid of what you would do to me."

We all laughed.

We lined up next to one another, kicked over a few small rocks to break the tension below us, then jumped.

My stomach did not leave my throat the whole way down. I don't know how, but I managed a scream past it.

We crashed into the water. It. Was. Cold!

My head popped up and saw that Lisette had already surfaced. Hanna came up shortly after.

We laughed and cheered while we treaded the water, shivering.

We swam to the shore and made our way back to the limo.

"Take the long way back!" Lisette told the driver.

We started our second bottle of champagne and stood up through the sunroof, taking in the sights of the capital of Olandia at night.

The architecture was baroque, glittered with various forms of technology. It was classical with a sense of progressivism. Hopefully, Jonathon and I would rule like that, holding onto some traditions while changing in some ways for the better.

We made it back to the castle, where all of us stumbled out of the limo, laughing. Jonathon stood at the top of the stairs, arms folded, smiling.

"Well, at least she is in *one* piece," he said.

He came down the stairs and picked me up into his arms.

"You. Are. So. Strong," I said, rubbing my face into his bicep.

He chuckled. "Oh, you are going to feel this in the morning. Good thing our wedding isn't until the afternoon."

CHAPTER 20

I WOKE UP THE NEXT MORNING WITH A KILLER HEADache. I tried to sit up, but the pounding worsened. I collapsed back onto my bed.

There was a light knock on my door. I responded with a groan.

Jonathon entered, chuckling. "I brought you some food and ibuprofen."

"God bless you," I said, popping the pills and downing my glass of water.

He sat on the bed next to me while I dug into my breakfast.

"You seemed like you had a lot of fun last night," he said, smiling.

"I really did. Hanna had me try some pretty terrifying things, but I found the courage to do them." I smiled back.

He raised an eyebrow. "Terrifying things?"

"She had us zipline over a lake and then jump into it from off the cliff."

His mouth dropped open. "Go you."

"Pretty sure it was just the alcohol." I chuckled.

He shook his head. "I don't think so. You have shown that you can do things that terrify you: risking your life to save others, spying on a dangerous man, dancing with me in public." We laughed at the last one.

I hugged him. "Thank you. I guess I will just keep doing what it is that I am doing." I pulled away, lying back onto the bed. "Just without so much alcohol."

Lisette was finishing up my makeup while Hanna was finishing up my hair. She had loosely twisted the sides and brought them together in a messy bun with baby's breath sprinkled throughout. She attached the veil under the bun.

I walked to the mirror and could not stop the smile from taking over my face. Lisette handed me my bouquet of white and navy blue roses.

I let out a deep breath. "All right, girls, let's do this!"

Since I had no father and King Olov was no longer with us, I chose Thomas to walk me down the aisle.

"Thank you," I whispered to him as we waited for my cue to enter the main hall.

"Absolutely, Ellena." He put his hand on my trembling one, clutching his arm.

The "Bridal Chorus" came on.

Here we go!

We started our painfully slow walk down the aisle. Jonathon's side was filled with people. Mine was sparse; it only contained those who had become my friends since coming here.

Jonathon came into view. He was in a white tux with a navy blue cummerbund, bow tie, and sash crossing his chest. The smile he was giving me almost made me melt onto the carpet leading up to the priest.

Thomas gave me to Jonathon, and I handed my bouquet to Hanna.

Jonathon and I took our places in front of the priest, facing each other while holding hands.

"You look beautiful," he mouthed to me.

"Thank you," I mouthed back, grinning.

As the preacher started addressing the congregation, I thought back over all that had happened the last several weeks. I had been hired to work at the palace, rose to the status of lady, embarrassed myself more times than I could count in front of the man I fell in love with, got kidnapped, was getting married, and was about to become queen.

"Jonathon, would you please recite your vows?" the priest said.

Jonathon started rubbing my knuckles. "Ellena … I love that I swept you off your feet during our first meeting."

I am sure everyone else thought that was a romantic sentiment; I, however, knew otherwise. I smiled, shaking my head at him.

He smiled and continued. "I knew from that first meeting that I had to get to know you more. I have not been disappointed at all with all that I have found out about you."

Here come the tears.

"I love your piercing green eyes, your smile. I love the way you laugh, your sense of humor. I love your selflessness, your bravery. I love the way you enjoy life to the fullest. I look forward to a lifetime of enjoying all of these things and learning about even more."

I blinked away the tears.

"And you, Lady Ellena," the priest said to me.

"Jonathon, I grew up seeing your face on magazines and newspapers. It *never* crossed my mind that I would be the one lucky enough to win your heart. These past several weeks, for me, have been a whirlwind. And I know that I could not have gone through any of it without you. I hope our lives calm down *just a little bit,* but if not, there is no one else that I would rather go through it with than you."

He squeezed my hands.

The rings were brought to us, and we put them on each other.

"By the power vested in me, I now pronounce you husband and wife."

We closed the distance between us and showed the congregation a sweet kiss.

They erupted in cheers.

Jonathon held up our hands, and they cheered even louder.

A chair was brought up behind me, and I took my place on it.

The room silenced.

The archbishop came up and placed an orb in my left hand and a scepter in my right. He went behind me, hovering my crown above my head.

"Do you, Ellena Larsson, swear to rule Olandia, according to her laws, with justice and mercy?"

"I, Ellena Larsson, do swear to rule Olandia, according to her laws, with justice and mercy."

"Do you swear to protect her from all threats, both foreign and domestic?"

"I do swear to protect her from all threats, both foreign and domestic."

"Do you swear to do all these things until your dying day?"

"I do swear to do all these things until my dying day."

I felt the crown placed onto my head. I took a deep breath.

He stood beside me and motioned for me to stand. "I present to you, Olandia, your queen. Queen Ellena Larsson."

The congregation erupted again.

The archbishop took the orb and scepter, and I grabbed Jonathon's outstretched arm. We walked down the aisle and out to the gardens, everyone else following behind.

My new crown made walking, let alone dancing, difficult. Needless to say, I only danced our first couple's dance. We spent most of our reception making our rounds to all our guests.

The party did not seem like it was winding down anytime soon when the sun began to set.

Jonathon took my hand and led me to the side of the castle. He moved some ivy that was crawling the wall and exposed a hidden door.

"We have secret passageways?" I gasped.

"Every good castle does." He chuckled.

He turned on the flashlight on his phone and led us through the dark stairway. It seemed to go on forever until we came to a door that opened onto the third floor.

"Sneaking away from our own reception, huh?" I asked.

He looked down at me with that same look I had seen only twice before. "We have talked to everyone that we needed to. Now, I want to be selfish. I am wanting to be alone with my wife." He gave me a smirk that made my legs feel like Jell-O.

My heart started thumping wildly in my chest.

He walked us to our new rooms. He stopped at the doorway and turned his body to face mine. He looked over my face, stroking it with his hand. He moved it up to the top of my head, taking off my crown, then his.

"Tonight, we are not king and queen. We are simply Jonathon and Ellena." He opened the doors and then scooped me up into his arms, his eye contact never breaking mine.

I woke up the next morning facing Jonathon, who was still asleep. The sheet was the only thing covering his perfect physique. I closed my eyes and smiled, thinking about the night before.

Jonathon began to stir. His eyes slowly opened. He immediately smiled at me.

"Good morning, beautiful," he said, holding my face and giving me a kiss.

"Good morning," I replied, smiling.

"Are you ready for a week away from here?"

"I am. Are you?"

"Absolutely."

We got dressed and packed our bags, then headed down for breakfast with the queen. I wondered how long it would take for meals to not feel so odd without King Olov there.

We said our goodbyes to Queen Leona and then headed for the waiting limo. Jonathon held my door open for me, then went to the other side and got in. He grabbed the newspaper from off his seat and read it aloud as we took off:

> Yesterday was a joyous day for the kingdom of Olandia. Our beloved King Jonathon and Lady Ellena were married, and she was crowned our queen. Quite a story for our Queen Ellena. She was raised in an orphanage, and because she was never adopted, she aged out and went to work at the palace. That's when the fairy tale began. She and King Jonathon fell in love. She was kidnapped and rescued by her prince charming and our beloved late King Olov. She rose through the ranks in record time and now serves our great country. I, for one, am looking forward to what she and King Jonathon have in mind for their reign. I cannot wait to see what becomes of our very own royal orphan.

This book was a dream I had years ago that revisited me off and on. I decided to put it down on paper and expand it. I hope you enjoyed reading it as much as I did writing it.

Lanelle Thomas is a wife and mother who is working on obtaining her bachelor's degree in Christian counseling from Liberty University. She hopes to use the knowledge she gains to help others navigate through this life. Now that her dream of becoming an author is a reality, she wants to help others escape this life through her writings. She lives with her husband, their four children, and their two furbabies in Grabill, Indiana.

Lightning Source UK Ltd.
Milton Keynes UK
UKHW042109230221
379286UK00001B/39

9 781480 899926